D0753796

PROFILE

FIRSTBORN SON: Hawk Stone

AGE: 35

STATS: Half Native American; tall, lean and muscular with vivid green eyes and shiny, shoulder-length hair

OCCUPATION: Cop

AREA OF EXPERTISE: Security

PERSONALITY: Wary but warm

FAVORITE SPORT: Lacrosse

MOST CHARMING CHARACTERISTIC: A roguish twinkle in his bright green eyes

BRAVEST ACT OF COURAGE: Saving a young boy from a crazed father

PREFERRED ROMANTIC SETTING: A quiet and cozy evening in front of a fireplace

GREATEST PASSION: Winning the heart of a beautiful, headstrong FBI agent

Dear Reader,

Once again, Silhouette Intimate Moments brings you six exciting romances, a perfect excuse to take a break and read to your heart's content. Start off with *Heart of a Hero,* the latest in award-winning Marie Ferrarella's CHILDFINDERS, INC. miniseries. You'll be on the edge of your seat as you root for the heroine to find her missing son—and discover true love along the way. Then check out the newest of our FIRSTBORN SONS, *Born Brave,* by Ruth Wind, another of the award winners who make Intimate Moments so great every month. In Officer Hawk Stone you'll discover a hero any woman—and that includes our heroine!—would fall in love with.

Cassidy and the Princess, the latest from Patricia Potter, is a gripping story of a true princess of the ice and the hero who lures her in from the cold. With *Hard To Handle,* mistress of sensuality Kylie Brant begins CHARMED AND DANGEROUS, a trilogy about three irresistible heroes and the heroines lucky enough to land them. Be sure to look for her again next month, when she takes a different tack and contributes our FIRSTBORN SONS title. Round out the month with new titles from up-and-comers Shelley Cooper, whose *Promises, Promises* offers a new twist on the pregnant-heroine plot, and Wendy Rosnau, who tells a terrific amnesia story in *The Right Side of the Law.*

And, of course, come back again next month, when the romantic roller-coaster ride continues with six more of the most exciting romances around.

Enjoy!

Leslie J. Wainger
Executive Senior Editor

Please address questions and book requests to:
Silhouette Reader Service
U.S.: 3010 Walden Ave., P.O. Box 1325, Buffalo, NY 14269
Canadian: P.O. Box 609, Fort Erie, Ont. L2A 5X3

BORN BRAVE

Ruth Wind

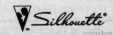

INTIMATE MOMENTS™

Published by Silhouette Books

America's Publisher of Contemporary Romance

If you purchased this book without a cover you should be aware that this book is stolen property. It was reported as "unsold and destroyed" to the publisher, and neither the author nor the publisher has received any payment for this "stripped book."

Special thanks and acknowledgment are given
to Ruth Wind for her contribution
to the FIRSTBORN SONS series.

This book is for my niece, Jessica Rae Hair, whose arrival in the world distracted me more than once—and gave me a good reason to get out and take a walk when I'd been at the computer too many hours. This one's for you, sweetie. Welcome to the world!

 SILHOUETTE BOOKS

ISBN 0-373-27176-X

BORN BRAVE

Copyright © 2001 by Harlequin Books S.A.

All rights reserved. Except for use in any review, the reproduction or utilization of this work in whole or in part in any form by any electronic, mechanical or other means, now known or hereafter invented, including xerography, photocopying and recording, or in any information storage or retrieval system, is forbidden without the written permission of the editorial office, Silhouette Books, 300 East 42nd Street, New York, NY 10017 U.S.A.

All characters in this book have no existence outside the imagination of the author and have no relation whatsoever to anyone bearing the same name or names. They are not even distantly inspired by any individual known or unknown to the author, and all incidents are pure invention.

This edition published by arrangement with Harlequin Books S.A.

® and TM are trademarks of Harlequin Books S.A., used under license. Trademarks indicated with ® are registered in the United States Patent and Trademark Office, the Canadian Trade Marks Office and in other countries.

Visit Silhouette at www.eHarlequin.com

Printed in U.S.A.

Bound by the legacy of their fathers, six Firstborn Sons are about to discover the stuff true heroes—and true love—are made of....

Hawk Stone: He will protect royal decoy Laurie Lewis with his life—if necessary. But how is this duty-bound cop supposed to suppress his vast hunger for the alluring undercover agent when they share luxury accommodations with *adjoining* bedroom doors?

Laurie Lewis: When she poses as a regal princess to bait dangerous kidnappers, this ambitious FBI agent vows to keep her mind on business—not pleasure. However, the heady sensation of her darkly handsome bodyguard's strong, muscular arms wrapped around her *is* awfully hard to resist....

Caleb Stone: Over the years, his son Hawk's way of life on the reservation shielded him from Caleb's dangerous profession. But has the time come for Caleb to pass his daunting legacy on to his Firstborn Son?

The Royal Feud: For more than a century, the heated battle between the royal Sebastiani and Kamal clans has left both kingdoms vulnerable to attack. Now the peacekeeping intervention of the Noble Men will either bring a long-awaited truce...or cause more bloodshed!

A note from award-winning novelist Ruth Wind,
author of over 15 romances for Silhouette Books:

Dear Reader,

I've rarely had as much fun with two characters as
I've had with Hawk Stone, a sexy Native American
cop, and Laurie Lewis, the tomboy from Nebraska who
wants only to prove herself in the world of FBI field
operations. One part of the fun, I have to admit, was
the whole angle of "dress-up"—it played right into my inner
six-year-old's most delicious wish, to be a princess. Only,
instead of doing it in my grandmother's blue chiffon robe
and a pair of plastic high heels from the toy department, I
got to play along with Laurie-as-Princess-Julia and wear
suits that cost a month's salary, Italian spectator pumps and
top-drawer evening gowns. I hope you'll let yourself go and
play along with us!

As much fun as the masquerade angle was to write in
Born Brave—the latest installment of FIRSTBORN SONS
from Intimate Moments—I have to admit my favorite part of
the book can be summed up in one word: Hawk. Charming
and wary, tough and vulnerable—not to mention drop-dead
gorgeous—Hawk is my kind of guy all the way. I loved
discovering the layers of him as we journeyed together—
what makes a man like this tick? What sets him apart? And
heavens—how did he learn to kiss like that?

I hope you'll enjoy getting away from it all with this
adventure. I know I did. As always, I love to hear from you
at samuel@rmi.net.

Ruth Wind

Chapter 1

The land west of Flagstaff, Arizona where Hawk Stone kept his horses was considered by many to be desolate. Too silent. Too lonely. Too austere. People looked at it and saw the endless, scrub-and-cactus-studded dun of the desert, and thought it empty.

Hawk knew it wasn't. He had always believed that the desert required a stillness from the viewer, a quiet within that allowed the call of the wind to echo. A care that allowed the multitude of creatures to peek out of their hiding places. It wasn't anywhere near empty of humans, either. He knew where to look for trailers tucked into the shelter of a low bluff, the doors always turned toward the east; knew the hidden pathways between the fields that led to a hogan, a corral, a weathered cabin.

Driving his pickup toward the family land on a late May afternoon, however, Hawk wondered if those other people had always been right. The open landscapes, bounded only by sky, by abrupt mesas rising up from the earth, by the odd outcropping of rocks, seemed to reflect the emptiness eating him up from within.

Everyone said he'd just had a shock, that time would ease the hollowness that dogged him every moment of every day. He'd believed them at first, had tried to keep going on with his normal routines. But the emptiness only grew, and at the advice of his sergeant, Hawk had finally taken a leave of absence from the police force two months ago, in an attempt to get his head together.

It wasn't helping. Instead, without work, without a routine to give shape to his days, he felt he was slowly disappearing, granules of his flesh, his body, his heart, all blowing away on some unseen wind, until soon there would be nothing left, only his bones, turning white beneath the sun.

And yet he could not seem to find time to go back. Every morning he rose with the intent of going back to the station, telling them he was ready to get on with life. Every evening, he found he had not done it yet, though he couldn't recall exactly what had been so pressing that this one small errand ended up getting pushed out of the way.

If not for the need to care for his horses, he might already have slipped away. Every day a boy from a neighboring family drove out to ride and feed and water the two Appaloosas that had once been Hawk's joy, but he had to bring the water in himself, carried in an enormous blue-green plastic container that took up the entirety of the truck bed. Just now, as he turned into the potholed dirt road that led to the horses, he could feel the weight of all those gallons of water sloshing from one side to the other.

There had once been a hogan here, but it had been burned when Hawk's mother died, as was customary. A small silver-and-red trailer, sufficient only for the odd overnight stay, crouched close against the hillside. Hawk saw the light inside before he noticed the elegant silver-blue sedan parked near a stand of scrub oak. He didn't recognize the car, but there was only one person it could be. He slowed.

A lone figure stood at the corral fence, feeding the spotted mares carrots he carried in his pockets for them. A tall, fit man with hair so silver it looked polished in the growing twilight. A true Westerner, but one who'd made good.

Hawk's father, Caleb Stone. Who heard the truck and turned slowly, lifting a hand in greeting.

Hawk parked, yanking the emergency brake with more force than he intended. It wasn't that he didn't like his father. He did. Caleb was a good man, and wise. But Hawk wasn't in the mood to see the compassion in those vivid green eyes. He didn't want to defend himself one more time against the worry of someone who loved him. Didn't want to make up excuses for why he just couldn't seem to get anything done these days.

"Hello, Son," Caleb said.

Hawk gave him a nod. "Don't have a lot of time, Dad, sorry to say. Gotta get back and take care of some business."

"That's fine, that's fine. I just wanted to talk to you a little bit."

Hawk sighed. "Look, I don't know who called you—" it could have been any number of aunts, un-

cles or cousins, all of whom had been fretting
''—but I'm all right. Really. I'm just not in the mood
for other people, okay?''

''Hear me out, Hawk. Ten minutes, and I swear I
won't say a word about your life. I'm kinda hoping I
can get you to do me a favor.''

Hawk rounded the truck and yanked open the gate
before he spoke. ''What kind of favor?''

''Why don't you go ahead and take care of your
business there, then come up to the trailer and I'll tell
you about it? I've got some coffee going.''

Caleb Stone was a stubborn man. If he wanted
Hawk's ear, he wouldn't give up until he got it. Hawk
gave a short nod. ''Be up in a sec.''

The horses ambled up to the fence, one moon-white
with freckles of black across her back, the other taller,
grayer, with a heavy black mane. They nuzzled his
head and his pockets—that was a horse for you, he
thought, always faithful. And he couldn't bear to dis-
appoint them. He fed them apples culled from the
stores in his kitchen in Flagstaff, delaying the moment
when he'd have to listen to his father.

It wasn't that Hawk was depressed or brooding or
any of those other terms people kept using. His partner had been killed, and Hawk had been unable to do
anything about it. Pure, simple, stupid. Like the
world. But if a man didn't spend time grieving the
loss of his best friend, if the world just looked normal
after something like that, what kind of world would
it be, anyway?

The cop psychiatrist he'd been forced to see had
asked him what he felt. And that was the trouble. He
didn't exactly *feel* anything. It was as if all the color
had been leached from the world. Not completely, just

like an old photo, the reds gone to pale orange, the blues a soft gray, the browns faded to barely discernable shades of dun.

Sooner or later, he figured the color would come back. It just took time.

Armored by this bit of reason, he walked through the gathering darkness, his boots crunching over the dried stalks of old weeds. Ten feet from the cabin he smelled the coffee and had to admit it had a powerful quality to it.

Inside, he joined his father at the white-and-gold Formica table tucked beneath the slat-covered window. Caleb had poured strong coffee into two battered ceramic mugs. Both men drank it the same way, with plenty of sugar, no cream.

"What's up?" Hawk asked.

Caleb measured him with sharp eyes. Hawk found himself remembering a time when he'd searched his father's strong face in vain for some evidence of himself. Only their eyes were the same. Caleb was an Anglo, square-jawed, with a beard he had to shave twice a day. He had blunt, square hands.

"You're thin," he said.

Hawk looked at this own hands, long and dark and graceful, like his mother's. He lifted a shoulder. "We aren't gonna talk about me, remember?"

Caleb considered that, then put his elbows on the table. "All right. Let's get to business, then. What do you know about Montebello?"

"You mean the island?" At his father's nod, he frowned. Sipped his coffee. "A little country in the Mediterranean, with one of those royal families that show up in the tabloids all the time. Fairly wealthy country, though I don't remember why. Oil?"

"Right. Oil, tourism, gems." Caleb took his time lifting his coffee, taking a sip, putting it back down. "I have a particular interest in Montebello, partly because I have some land and investments there, and partly because King Marcus is an old friend."

"A king is your old friend." Hawk said it as a statement. He never had known exactly what his father did for his obviously lucrative income, but had long suspected that Caleb was a mercenary of some sort. He had the haleness and strength, the cunning intelligence, the shrewd instincts required of such men, and Hawk knew it had been hard for Caleb to come home after Vietnam. "How'd you get to be buddies with a king, Dad?"

"Some years ago, there was a rebellion. The king was only crown prince then, and he asked for help, which some of my associates and I were happy to give. He rewarded us with land. Now he needs help again."

"With?" Hawk could not imagine how he was going to fit into this.

"Tensions in the area have recently skyrocketed. King Marcus's son and heir—Lucas—went down in a private plane over the Rockies three months ago and his body has not been recovered. The king is understandably grief-stricken over the loss of his son, but matters have been complicated by his daughter Julia, who recently announced that she is pregnant."

"That seems like a good thing—a baby to help them all get over the loss."

Caleb allowed an ironic smile. "Indeed it would be, under normal circumstances. Unfortunately, she has admitted that the baby's father is Rashid Kamal, the heir of Tamir's sheikdom. Are you familiar with the tensions between the two countries?''

''Not really. I remember hearing about it. Not quite as serious as the Israelis and Palestinians, but a long, old feud, right?''

''Yes. That's enough to know for now, because it gets complicated enough here. Rashid, the eldest son of Sheik Ahmed Kamal, Tamir's king, is also missing and presumed dead.''

''Ah.'' In spite of himself, Hawk felt a curious stirring of interest. ''So there are two missing crown princes and a princess who is carrying what amounts to the heir of both crowns.''

''Exactly.''

''So where do I come into this?''

''Sheik Ahmed believes that King Marcus has something to do with his son's disappearance—the sheik is crazed with grief and appears to be ready to do anything to take Princess Julia and the baby she's carrying. King Marcus is also a little crazed and can't believe his son is dead. There have been two bombings in Montebello and a kidnapping attempt on Princess Julia.''

''And the Sheik's behind them?''

''We don't really know. He swears he's not involved, and in fact is furious at being accused. One of the terrorists who set the second bomb claimed he was hired by Kamal, but the sheik is still insisting he did not do it. We're not sure what to think. Security has been stepped up around the palace and the royal family.'' Caleb stood up to pour a second cup of coffee, topped off Hawk's cup and sat back down. ''We're going to set a trap by sending the princess out on a publicity tour of the U.S. There have been reports that she's missing, too, and we can kill two birds with one stone this way.''

Hawk frowned. ''That seems unwise, especially if she's pregnant. What if they succeed?''

''Exactly. It won't really be the princess.'' His father smiled. ''There's a woman on the administrative side of the FBI who is a dead ringer for Julia. She's been pulled to take the assignment, her first.''

''A civilian?'' Hawk was plainly disapproving.

''No. Not at all. She's had agent training, but hasn't yet been in the field. For that reason, I want to be sure she's got the best possible guard. I want someone with the instincts of a cop, who also understands the role of a royal bodyguard.''

Hawk had done ambassadorial duty in the service. ''Me.''

Caleb nodded.

Hawk rubbed his thumbnail over the white-and-gold pattern of the tabletop, no answer forming inside of him. No reaction, one way or the other. ''I don't think I'm your man, sir. No offense. I just don't seem to have the instincts for it anymore.''

''I thought that's what you'd say.'' His father rose, and Hawk thought that would be that. He was aware of a faint sense of disappointment, mixed with a bigger helping of relief.

But Caleb only added more sugar to his cup. ''I promised your aunt I'd look out for you once she was gone.'' Heavily, he sat down and peered hard at Hawk. ''I know I wasn't the best father, Son, but I've been a father figure to enough men that I can see when one is wandering lost inside himself.'' His jaw tightened. ''I haven't slept for thinking of you, and what I'm hoping is that you'll take my advice for once in your life. Trust me.''

Hawk raised his head, the relief even stronger now. Relief that this might be the lifeline he instinctively knew he needed, a way to get back on track. "I'm listening."

"Sometimes, Hawk," the older man said quietly, "you just need a hand once in a while. I'm offering mine. Will you do this for me?"

"Why not one of the FBI undercover units?"

Caleb's gaze was steady and clear. "Because I asked that you be allowed to do it. Will you? As a favor to me?"

Hawk felt a stir. "Yeah, I'll do it," he said, surprising himself. An image of catching a lifeline— even rope burn on his hand to prove it—flashed through his mind. "Tell me what needs to be done."

Two thousand miles away, Laurie Lewis was alone in the administrative offices of the FBI, online and on the telephone at once, looking for a secondary cover for an agent who had just had to flee an assignment and now huddled in a bistro in Paris, looking for a way back to safety. "You there, David?" she said.

"Yeah," said the haggard voice on the line. "What's up?"

"I've got your answer. At 10:00 a.m., follow procedure C-087 and you should be hooked up."

The agent let go of a heavy breath. "Thanks, doll. I owe you."

"You all do, honey. You all do." She broke the connection, then stretched, wondering with a little ache of longing what it would be like to be out there, in a dark Paris bistro, waiting for a lifeline. Or better yet, what it would be like to pull off an assignment and maybe save a life or even a country.

Beyond the windows, a heavy spring rain poured out of a dark sky, exaggerating the taillights of the cars in the streets and giving the whole, gardenlike section of the city a thick wash of green. Around her in the office, other administrative personnel answered phones and questions, some mundane, some dull, some exciting like the one she'd just completed. Laurie's specialty was identities and itineraries, but she remembered working the secretarial angles, hoping for the chance to be sitting in the seat she now occupied.

She was good at her job. There were parts of it that made her feel like a kid with a secret decoder ring, but she recognized that her talent made it possible for others to go out in the field with a good deal more confidence.

"Ms. Lewis, do you have a moment?"

Tugged from her reverie, Laurie looked up to see Timothy Lake, her immediate superior, a tall man with a grizzling wreath of hair around a pate that shone in the fluorescent light overhead. "Sure, Mr. Lake." She tugged off her headset and smoothed her skirt, following him down a hushed and carpeted hallway.

In her conservative pumps, she was five-ten, a good three inches taller than he, and he looked up. "Good work on the Talmud case, by the way. Everyone has commented on it. You'll be receiving an official commendation come August."

Laurie grinned. "Really? That's great! Thank you!"

"We're going to need your help with another matter today, however."

"Oh?" The "we" caught her attention. Which "we" would that be?

But before she could form the question, he stopped in front of a door that Laurie knew led to a conference room. She gave him a quizzical look, and he smiled. "Don't be nervous, all right?"

"That helped," she muttered as he led the way in, through a secretarial room, then a small anteroom to a vast, windowless area furnished with various electronic equipment, including a wall of flickering television screens, each showing a different scene. The long, mahogany table in the center was flanked with three or four of the highest-ranking members of the organization, along with a few other people she didn't recognize. All of them wore the conservative suits that made up Washington business attire.

All but one. Sitting apart from the others was a man she assumed must be an agent. He wore a pair of well-worn jeans and a red corduroy shirt that brought out the glossy darkness of his shoulder-length hair. He stared directly at Laurie with a measuring, serious expression that was not particularly friendly. His eyes were a vivid green, startling in the dark, Native American face.

Wow, she thought. She'd have to remember to tell her roommate, Tanya, about this guy. Tanya lived for exotically gorgeous men and would drool over Laurie's description of this one.

"Gentlemen," said Mr. Lake. "This is Laurie Lewis."

A dark-haired man in his fifties was the first to speak. "Remarkable."

Another man, who Laurie recognized as Caleb Stone, her liaison on a developing case in the Mediterranean, stood and extended his hand. Stone was an expert on the country of Montebello and had been working with Laurie for the past month on a project documenting the royal family. "Please sit down, Ms. Lewis. We have a matter of some urgency to discuss with you."

She took the chair he pulled out for her, uncomfortably aware of the scrutiny and low murmurs of some of the others. What was going on? "Is there a problem?"

"Yes," Mr. Stone said. "But it's something we're hoping you'll be able to help us with."

"I'll be glad to try."

"Ladies and gentlemen," Mr. Stone said, "Ms. Lewis has been a key research specialist for our agents dealing with the Montebello-Tamir situation. She put together the original research documents for our agents, and has written more than a dozen briefs. Ms. Lewis, will you tell the others what some of those briefs covered?"

"Of course." Aloud, she listed some of the more important dossiers she'd logged, and the three undercover operations she'd helped to arrange. She was proud of her work on it. "I would say I'm one of three or four experts on the Sebastiani history."

Stone smiled. "So you are, then, quite familiar with the habits of Princess Julia?"

"Of course. She recently confessed to being pregnant with Sheik Rashid Kamal's child." Laurie had been moved by the young princess's story. "And there are some rumors that she's missing, which is leading to even more volatility in the area."

"Ms. Lewis," said the first man who'd spoken. "Please look at the screen."

A picture of Princess Julia, obviously taken at a charity function of some sort, was called up on one of the monitors. She was a tall, slim woman with thick dark hair and milk-smooth skin. Her suit was an ecru linen that likely would have cost half Laurie's monthly salary. The Italian leather pumps she wore would have consumed the other half. "That was taken in London two and a half years ago, I believe," Laurie said. "Near the end of her marriage." Julia had been more or less in seclusion since the highly publicized divorce.

"Yes." The man zoomed in on her face, a remarkably clear focus. "Now please look at this."

The second picture was one of Laurie in a beige wool suit she'd found for a song in the bargain basement of Saks, a suit she thought looked great on her. The man zoomed in on her own face, and Laurie suddenly saw what she was meant to see. "Wow. Quite a resemblance," she said mildly, trying to cover the sudden rush of excitement that zipped through her. "I never noticed before."

"It's not just a resemblance," said Caleb Stone. "It's uncanny. We've been over dozens of tapes, and you've been under observation for several weeks. Your body movements are much more American and athletic, and your hair is lighter and longer than hers, but the facial resemblance is truly remarkable."

"And?" she asked as coolly as possible.

"According to your file, you passed your field training with the highest marks in the class. You're certified for weapons and undercover work, and have recently been listed for a commendation. Is that all correct?''

"Yes, sir." She folded her hands, discovering her fingers were ice-cold. Her heart was beating so loudly she was afraid the others might hear it and think she was not at all suited for whatever project they were obviously leading up to.

A silence fell. The side-by-side pictures of the princess and Laurie hung in mute testimony, and everyone looked at them without comment for a long moment. Nervously, Laurie glanced toward the agent type against the wall and found that he was regarding her again with the same impassive, slightly hostile gaze. She scowled at him. Did he think she couldn't do it?

There were obviously those with doubts. She saw it in their eyes—most especially in the eyes of those who knew her. They *didn't* think she could do it. Three times in the past year she'd been passed over for an entry-level field position.

Suddenly, that made her angry. She had earned the highest marks in her class. A commendation for putting together the overview intelligence for other agents. Four promotions in eighteen months—but every last one of them had been in an administrative capacity. She was making more money than she'd ever expected to earn at this age, but she literally ached to test herself in the field.

Worse, Laurie knew exactly why they had never given her the chance. For months she'd been studying the female agents, some younger than she, and recognized that they all shared a quality she simply lacked: edge. Laurie Lewis, tomboy from Nebraska, was tough and scrappy, but she was too nice.

Feeling the disapproval gathering among her superiors, Laurie inclined her head. "May I speak frankly?"

Mr. Stone turned. He was her only ally in the room, the only one she could count on. She suspected he might have been the one who'd managed to get her in this chair in the first place. "Please, Ms. Lewis."

She stood, utilizing her height to advantage. "I have been with this agency for seven years, two as an intern before I even left college. In that time, I've learned the organization from the inside out. I bet I know things that none of you know. I am absolutely certain I'm one of the best that's ever been at certain aspects of field work."

They listened impassively. Unmoved.

"When Jenna Richardson brought down the assassin in Morocco last year, she used my research and the persona I created. When the team for Milan was exposed, it was my work that kept them from getting blown up two days later. I can do this."

"Ms. Lewis," said John Norman, director of overseas operations, "your earnestness is admirable, but—"

"Pardon me," Laurie said, lifting a hand. In sudden inspiration, she plucked a pencil from the table and walked in her strong American, tomboyish style to the front of the room.

"I'm tired of being passed over because everyone thinks I'm too nice. Nice doesn't necessarily equal stupid." She twisted her hair into a knot and secured it with the pencil, then unbuttoned her suit jacket and tossed it over a chair.

At the front of the room, she turned her back and took a long deep breath, using the time to pull in the details of Princess Julia. She straightened her spine imperceptibly, smoothed her skirt over her hips and imagined she wore long nails on fingers adorned with a diamond. Then she tugged slightly on her silk tank top to show a hint more cleavage.

She turned around and, imagining a basket of fruit balanced precariously on the top of her head, walked to the microphone. In a soft, accented and throatier voice than she ordinarily used, she said, "On behalf of my father and my country, I am so pleased to be here today." She flashed the slightly trembling, elusive smile that was such a trademark of the princess, a smile that intrigued millions, and knew immediately that her gift for mimicry had allowed her to capture it perfectly.

The response was immediate—a laugh, then a quick flurry of clapping. "Well done," said Timothy Lake.

Caleb Stone winked at her.

Only the agent on the sidelines seemed unimpressed. Laurie inwardly rolled her eyes. She didn't need his approval.

"I'd say we've found our operative," Caleb said. "James, will you come up here? Laurie, I'd like you to meet my son, James Stone. He'll be posing as your bodyguard. I've asked for him specifically since, as well as the training of a soldier and police officer, he has had experience with ambassadorial tours."

Oh, great. Laurie struggled to keep her expression neutral as the man got to his feet and walked up to where they stood. He moved with the alert reserve she associated with animals in the wild—a wariness around his eyes that showed nothing, a readiness in the shoulders when he halted and held out his hand in an almost wry offering, she had the definite sense that he disapproved of her. "How're you doing?" he said.

Laurie blinked. His voice was low and musical, echoing with a resonance she had never heard before, a depth and richness that just didn't seem to mesh with those feral, catlike green eyes. "You have your father's eyes," she said, looking from one to the other.

"So we've been told."

She wondered if he would ever read aloud to her. She could close her eyes and listen to that voice rolling over her like a hand—

"We have a lot to do," said a short, well-dressed woman in sturdy shoes. Her diction was very precise and measured, her voice thinner and higher than Laurie would have expected. "The tour is going to start in two days, and we have to get you ready, young lady."

Caleb stepped back with a smile. "This is Ms. Watson. She'll be your consultant."

"Oh!" Laurie exclaimed. They were starting *now*. "I need to make a couple of calls."

"You can do that later. And it's Mrs., not Ms." The consultant took Laurie's arm. "I'm going to give you a crash course in manners and protocol, as well as supervise your shopping." From beside her chair, she took an enormous leather handbag and settled it over her substantial elbow. "Come along, young man, you're coming, too."

Chapter 2

Hawk had watched the transformation with a sense of amazement. He'd noticed the princess—what red-blooded American male hadn't?—when her likeness had been plastered on every tabloid in America. Her marriage had been news on the gossip circuit, and the camera loved her mysterious smile, those shy but somehow come-hither eyes, the delectably female walk he was heartily pleased to know European women had not given up.

In a million years he wouldn't have seen *that* in the sturdy, healthy woman who'd come into the room, and he was a man who prided himself on pegging people—it had been his job, after all, for a long time, both as a soldier and a cop.

Laurie Lewis, the young woman who'd been led into the room, looked like a million secretaries all over America—clean, honest, organized. In fifty years, she would have a hefty bosom and lace-up shoes and still be running an office or a school or something, serene in her absolute indispensability. Right now, she was a perfect Wisconsin type—milk-fed, farm-raised Americana all the way. Straight white teeth and big blue eyes and an earnestness that was nearly painful.

And when she'd transformed herself, with the toss of a jacket and a pencil stuck in her hair like Wilma Flintstone, Hawk had been just a teeny bit ashamed of himself at the way he'd rushed to judge—and dismiss—her. Why had he been so quick to discount her abilities?

The question nagged him faintly over the next two hours like a sore toe, not really noticeable until he kicked it. Which somehow he kept doing, despite his best efforts.

Mrs. Watson had whisked them off to a dizzying series of hushed, carpeted boutiques, opened after hours on a rainy weekend night just for them. Now, two hours later, Hawk was beginning to get irritated and hungry, and really didn't want yet another parade of evening gowns or suits or cocktail dresses. Who even knew there existed distinctions between cocktail and evening?

He heard his stomach growl and wondered darkly why the hell he'd agreed to this nonsense. Laurie and Mrs. Watson were conferring on the choice of egg-shell or ecru for a suit. Both garments looked white to him. Laurie frowned, tugging the current jacket the smallest bit, then went back into the dressing room. His partner had had a word for women like her: *plastic*. As in Barbie doll. As in cute enough, but nothing inside.

She was plenty nice to look at. Thick hair, a pretty

face with lovely blue eyes. Excellent lips. And no
Barbie doll would be complete without a set of absolutely gorgeous legs—long and shapely, leading to
a rear end that wasn't too big or too small, but just
right. But then, it was Barbie's job to look cute,
wasn't it?

After a moment, Laurie swirled out of the dressing
room again, this time clad in a white evening gown.
It swooped low in front, revealing cleavage in the
most elegantly stimulating way he could imagine—
rich babes always had that down pat. He could only
imagine what sort of bra made everything sit up so
nicely.

No, maybe he didn't really want to imagine that.

"What do you think?" she said, turning this way
and that. "The princess wears a lot of white, but I
gotta say it's not making me real happy to imagine
how I'll keep from spilling something on myself
every time."

"It's nice," he said, then appealed to Mrs. Watson.
"Can we take a break to eat sometime soon?"

"Oh, of course, of course! How thoughtless of
me!" She brushed the skirt of the dress with a familiar, motherly hand, and Laurie jumped, sending
Hawk a funny look that made her seem a lot more
human suddenly. And he realized she was brand-new
at this, excited by the drama of playing a princess—
hell, it would be fun for any woman, wouldn't it?

But the point wasn't to have fun. The princess had
been targeted by kidnappers, for Pete's sake. Hawk
had a feeling his job as bodyguard might be a tough
assignment, and he'd be damned if she would play
bubblehead with his blessing. Once this business of
dress-up was finished, he intended to go over the rest

of the job so she didn't end up getting herself killed. Not on his watch.

"I'm starving, too," she said over her shoulder. "Does hamburger sound good to you? I know a great place. Onion rings as big as your fist, I swear."

"No hamburgers for you, young lady. Not until this is over. The princess eats like a lady. That's how she keeps herself a nice size eight," the consultant stated.

"Ah, but she's pregnant!" Laurie patted her flat stomach in the mirror. "Surely she'll get to eat a little more than usual."

"A little more. But no hamburgers. We'll dine in your suite. I'll have room service prepare something elegant for all of us."

"Suite?"

"Oh, yes!" Mrs. Watson said. "I'll have the manicurist meet us there." She scowled at Laurie's hands. "Those nails will never do."

"Acrylics?" Laurie asked. Her face lit up. "I always wanted to try them."

Hawk wanted to roll his eyes and barely restrained himself. All at once the lurking depression descended, like a bear sitting on his chest, squeezing out all the air in his lungs and deadening his emotions. Fake nails. He couldn't think of anything more useless. Long nails, period. Painted nails, painted faces, fancy gowns—none of it had any meaning to him. What was the point?

He felt weary and grimy and in need of a long, hot shower and that big hamburger Laurie mentioned. The atmosphere of the dressing room seemed oppressively opulent—the kind of false world that had no meaning anywhere outside a small, exclusive group he'd never had any interest in joining. Not for him the life of canapés and polite chitchat and evening gowns.

Give him jeans, a good pair of boots and a horse to ride under an open sky anytime.

"Hey, are you all right?" Laurie asked. She put her hand on his shoulder, and he just managed to avoid jerking away—something she obviously noticed, because she suddenly sank down in a crouch, the skirt of the white gown billowing out around her, and looked into his eyes. "You don't look great."

He glanced away. "I'm all right. Long trip, that's all."

"Well," she said, voice low with conspiracy. "I'll make sure you get a hamburger no matter what—but only if you let me have a bite."

He couldn't summon an answering smile, though he knew he should. He nodded. "Let's just get her to get us out of here."

Laurie sobered. "Sure." She squeezed his shoulder and straightened. A hint of some sunny, lemony scent came from her hair, a bright yellow note in the dullness of his mood. He let it in, something real to cling to for a few minutes.

Scrambling into a pair of jeans—they'd finally let her go by her apartment to pick up a few things—Laurie heaved a sigh of relief. Pumps and suits and understated silk were all very fine and well for work, but nothing could beat a good pair of old jeans for pure comfort. Pulling on an old Creighton sweatshirt, she wandered out of the opulent bedroom of the presidential suite of a very posh old hotel, and into the common sitting room.

Mrs. Watson was momentarily absent, and Laurie

was amazed to realize how glad she was not to see the woman for five minutes. "Where'd she go?" she asked, unwrapping one of her favorite things—a chocolate Tootsie roll pop.

Hawk sat on the couch, flipping through channels like every man in the universe. "Out to strong-arm a manicurist, I think."

"She's a dying breed." Laurie stuck the sucker in her mouth and slumped in a wing chair, then pulled her hair into a ponytail and secured it with a scrunchy. "The commandant."

"She gets the job done." Without looking at her, he flipped to an all-news station and let it stay there. "First assignment and everything."

He sounded faintly censorious, and Laurie frowned. "Do you have reservations about my ability to do this job? I'm not much into hints and veiled asides."

He lifted his shoulders. "I don't know." He looked at her. "I don't know you, but you seem pretty young and cheerleaderish for this kind of job."

Ow. Maybe she didn't like his brand of honesty, after all. "Cheerleaderish? Doesn't that mean enthusiastic, energetic, all those things?"

"*Earnest* and *peppy* were the words I was thinking of."

Jeez, he was nice looking. Brooding men who took themselves too seriously were totally not her type, but it was hard to miss how gorgeous this one was. His hair fell on his shoulders like a sweep of mink, shiny and thick and touchable, and his face was like something out of a painting. She had managed to adjust to his eyes a little—that startling green—but nothing was going to make the allure of that voice any less thrilling, not in a million years.

"You know," she said with a sigh, "I've been fighting that stereotype my whole life. I really get tired of it."

He flipped through three channels, paused on another news station, then looked at her. "Tell the truth. Were you a cheerleader?"

Laurie concentrated on the lollipop for a moment, then conceded. "Yes. My brothers all played football. It was the least I could do." She lifted a shoulder. "I wasn't all that great. Does that help?"

"I don't know. How bad were you?"

"Bad. The only reason they let me do it was because one of my brothers was the star quarterback that year."

He smiled the faintest bit. "What, you couldn't kick high enough?"

"Oh, I could kick fine. It was the coordination thing I had trouble with. And I hated the uniforms, those stupid little sweaters."

"Funny, I remember something else about cheerleader uniforms." The smile was a little more genuine now, and he held up a thumb and finger. "Skirts this big."

Laurie laughed. "What I really wanted was to play football, actually. I'd been playing tackle with my brothers all my life, and it seriously irked me that they wouldn't even let me try out for kicker."

Something like interest crossed his face. "No kidding."

"No. And let me tell you, I would have been much better at it than cheerleading." She leaned back in the oversize chair, propping her heels on the ottoman. "Did you play sports in school?"

"Sure. Basketball, wrestling, track."

"Did girls play any of those sports?

"They had their own basketball and track teams."

"Humph." She was tempted to bite into her sucker, and forced herself not to. "I think I'm jealous of girls now, not just getting to play sports, but really being encouraged to be athletic. I missed that whole thing."

"They still can't play football."

"It's getting better, though. We're starting to see some girls on guy teams. Women's basketball, women boxers—all those great commercials on television about women athletes. Don't you think?"

Hawk shook his head. "It's better, yeah, but the day a woman can play side by side with a man at anything is still a long way off."

"Can or is allowed?"

"Allowed." He flipped and stopped at the sports channel. "You notice there aren't women joining up to play men's basketball—that they created a whole new league for the women who are good enough to play professionally."

"True."

"It's a long time before there'll be girl football teams, babe. Longer still until there are females on male teams."

"Maybe," she conceded, and smiled. "Then again, who knew fifteen years ago that there would be a Woman's National Basketball Association?"

"Are you always this cheerful?"

"Pretty much," she said with a grin. "Are you always this grouchy?"

"I'm not grouchy. Just realistic."

"That's what you all say."

There was a quick knock on the door, and Mrs.

Watson sailed in with a room service cart and waiter, plus a thin, dark girl in tow. "Here we are," she sang out, "food and manicurist all at once. Young lady," she said to Laurie, "I want you...let's see...right there by the window. That will be sufficient light for you, won't it, Cheryl?"

"Yes, ma'am." She scurried over to the table and put down her metal suitcase.

Mrs. Watson peeked under the silver domes of the food cart, nodded her satisfaction and tipped the man generously. "Thank you. That will be all."

Laurie caught Hawk's eye and grinned. To her satisfaction, he could not quite repress the amusement shining in his eyes, and his grin, while reluctant, was real. "Much better," she said, and joined the manicurist at the table. "Can I have them wildly long?"

"As long as you want, miss! I can even put some jewels on them. Would you like that?"

"She would not," Mrs. Watson declared. "And nothing garish on the length." She carried a covered plate to Laurie's side and took off the lid with a flourish, revealing a small green salad, artfully and lovingly arranged, alongside a plain chicken breast. "Probably a French manicure would be best."

Laurie stared at the skimpy serving on the plate and sighed. With a small, stubborn scowl, she said, "I have my justifications, which I'd be glad to share with you later, but I want to paint the nails."

Mrs. Watson drew herself up. "I don't think so."

"*Julia*," Laurie said with significance, "likes colored nails."

"Oh, very well. Colors it is then."

Laurie smiled at the manicurist. "Red today, I think."

From the couch, Hawk said, "Make sure you can still operate small equipment easily. If you catch my meaning."

At first she didn't, and frowned at him in puzzlement as he uncovered the most gorgeous, enormous hamburger in the world. The smell of fried onions filled the room. He looked up at her, glanced at the manicurist, who had her back to him. Using his hand to make a gun, he shot at her.

"Oh!" Laurie said. "Right."

After dinner, there were more lessons in etiquette, most of which Laurie already knew. It was no exaggeration to say she was one of the agency experts on the feuding Sebastianis and Kamals, and she'd put in hundreds of hours of research in protocol, royal and state, in women's roles in the two societies, and just about every other level of the case.

What she worried about was acting the part of the princess so authentically that no one would ever suspect she wasn't the real thing. After Mrs. Watson retired, Laurie paced the common room of the suite, a book on her head, trying to be conscious of her arms and hands, which she—as Laurie—used freely and exuberantly. The princess was much more subdued.

It helped, actually, to have the red-painted nails. They gave her hands an elegant look, lengthening her fingers, making her aware of the way she moved those hands, how she handled things. She practiced picking things up—a cup out of a saucer, a shawl from the back of a chair, a quarter that had to be slid across the surface of the table rather than plucked up as Laurie was used to doing.

Out of the corner of her eye, she was aware of

Hawk, still sitting on the couch, his legs now propped up on the ottoman. On his feet were well-worn, lovingly tended cowboy boots with new heels. Noticing them, she said in the princess's voice, "Are you a horseman, sir? I have a pair of lovely Arabians, though of course I ride English, not western."

He looked at her as if he wasn't sure how he should respond. In her normal voice, Laurie said, "I'm just getting into character. Help me out here, will you?"

He leaned back, his long dark hands folded together over his flat belly. "All right. I have a pair of Appaloosas."

"Oh, yes! A very western sort of horse. Lovely." Laurie wondered if the princess would know the very American lore of the breed, and decided to use it. She was known as an ardent horsewoman. "They were prized by the Nez Percé Indians, I believe, who used them to hold off the U.S. Cavalry for quite some time."

His brows lifted. "Pretty good."

She practiced sitting, the book still on her head. "What do you like about the breed, Mr. Stone?"

"They're versatile," he said. "Haven't had all the uniqueness bred out of them, like so many these days—including your Arabians, which are fine horses, but a little high-strung."

"Indeed. And Appaloosas are not high-strung?"

"No, they're like dogs—they're loyal and want to please and they don't mind a little hard work." He inclined his head. "I like the way they look."

Laurie took the book off her head. As herself she said, "I like their eyes. They have human eyes."

"You have horses?"

"Not now. I had one growing up."

"On a farm?"

Laurie smiled at him. "Yes. Is it that obvious?"

"You're pretty wholesome."

"Eew. Cheerleader and wholesome in one night. I think I need to work on my image a bit." A little worried, she frowned. "Are you buying the transformation to the princess, though? That's the important thing."

For a moment, his jeweled eyes came alive, glittering and warm and *human* somehow, which made her realize how much was usually hidden beneath them. "Yeah, sweetheart, I'm buying it. You don't have anything to worry about on that level."

"What level should I worry about?"

He lifted a shoulder. "Let's go over that tomorrow, all right? I'm going to turn in."

"All right." She stood as he did, and held out her hand. "It's going to be very pleasant working with you, James."

He hesitated, then briefly clasped her hand. His fingers were warm and strong. "It's Hawk. Only my father ever calls me James. It was his father's name."

"Good night, Hawk."

At the door to his bedroom, he turned. "It's not gonna be pleasant, Laurie. I'm a hard-nosed cop, and by tomorrow at this time, you'll hate my guts."

"No, I don't hate anybody. It's your job to be hard."

He made a noncommittal noise and gave her a nod. "Night."

Chapter 3

Hawk shut the door on Miss Sun and Smiles with a sense of weariness. He undressed to his shorts, got in bed and turned out the lights. And lay there.

And lay there.

Rain pattered on the long windows, and every so often there was a distant roll of thunder. It was a sound he liked, having grown up in the desert where rain was more precious than rubies, but it brought him no comfort tonight. Each rumble only seemed a portent of disaster.

He'd believed that a change of scene might be just what the doctor ordered to snap him out of his funk, but lying in a rented bed, amid the false opulence of Washington, he only felt more disconnected than ever. He longed for his horses, the smell of the desert, the shine of the moon on a cloudless night.

Nah, that was a lie. He did love his horses and the desert, but this emptiness had been sucking him under there, too. This wasn't a problem of location. It was a problem of timing.

Time. All he wanted in the world was to go back in time, fix things, rearrange them so that everything now would be the way it was supposed to be.

He got up, donned the heavy terry-cloth robe supplied by the hotel, and went to the window. Staring down at the wet streaks of car lights below, he played with the fantasy of going back in time. What if a genie appeared and granted his wish?

Which moment in time would he pick to change?

Would he choose to go back to the night eight months ago when one of his oldest, best friends had taken his usual path home from work and been killed by a drunk driver? Or would he want to choose the brilliant, cold January afternoon six months ago when his partner was killed in a domestic violence dispute before Hawk could do a damned thing?

Or hell, maybe he'd just have to go all the way back in time to the year he was eight and his mother had been killed by a fall from a horse.

Decisions, decisions.

He didn't know why his mother had been on his mind so much lately. It had been a long time ago, after all. He didn't know if a boy ever really got over missing a mother taken from him too soon, but as these things went, he'd done all right. His mother's family had swarmed in with love and warmth to take care of him. He'd never felt left out, never felt to be less than his cousins. And later, when the family moved to Flagstaff for the work his uncle could find there, Hawk had even been given the chance to know his father, Caleb. He had adored the man, thinking him dashing and dangerous and exciting on his trips home from mysterious travels that took him all over the world. As a boy, Hawk had often wanted to go with his father, but Caleb had insisted—rightly, as it turned out—that Hawk would be better served living with his Navajo relatives until he was grown. Caleb took a house in Flagstaff, where he lived whenever he was in the States, and Hawk stayed with him there when he could.

Funny, Hawk thought now, staring at the darkness. Caleb never had married. As far as Hawk knew, he'd never really had a serious relationship except with Hawk's mother. Caleb's heart had been broken— twice—by Lorena Dovefeather. The first time when he was eighteen, a blue-collar boy in love with an Indian girl who was forbidden to marry him when he was drafted into the army. She'd promised to write. She never had.

Caleb never saw her again. The next he heard of her, she had been killed in an accident, and she'd left a child—his child—in the care of her relatives. It was when Caleb traveled home to Arizona that he'd learned Lorena had named her son for his father, a gesture of love that broke his heart so entirely that it had never healed.

Ancient history. All of it ancient. Hawk closed his eyes and pressed his forehead against the window, wishing only for the blankness of sleep. Instead, behind his eyelids flickered images—a wet road and a drunk's bad braking, and the body of Abe Jaramillo in his coffin. Another coffin, this one closed, containing the body of his partner, John Martinez. A sunny, cold January day, and shouts and a child—there had been a four-year-old in the room—sobbing and screaming, and trying to get the gun away from his dad. Hawk dived for the kid as John leveled his gun at the father and shots rang out. Hawk grabbed the boy and held his head to his chest as the man fell, as John fell, as the woman started to scream. He drew and fired as the woman fell, too....

A disaster. A disaster. He went over it and over it and over it and it never got better. What if he'd fired first? What if the woman hadn't screamed? What if Hawk had let the boy get killed? Would John still be alive?

A knock sounded at his door. "Hawk, there's a phone call for you."

He hadn't even heard the phone ring, and realized that it hadn't rung in here, but in the other room, on another line. "I'm sleeping," he called out.

Laurie stuck her head around the door. "I'm pretty sure it's your father. He asked for James. Do you want me to tell him to call back tomorrow?"

Hawk turned, considering. "No," he said with a sigh. "You'll be back in three seconds. He doesn't give up."

"Okay. I'll just tell him you're coming, and get out of the way."

Her lemony scent was stronger now, and as he came out of the dark into the warmly lit sitting area, he saw that she had just come from the shower. Her dark, wet hair lay on her shoulders, combed away from her face. Her bathrobe was floor-length, dark blue with moons and stars all over it. She looked about sixteen.

She pointed to the phone and started gathering up a stack of notes and scattered pieces of paper. "This will only take a minute," he said. "Don't stop what you're doing."

"You sure?"

He nodded and picked up the receiver. "This is Hawk."

"Hey, Son. Are you settling in all right with Ms. Lewis?"

"It's fine."

"Well, listen. There's been a serious attempt to kidnap the princess, the real one, and we're taking her into protective custody right now."

Hawk frowned. "Who is it?"

"We've believed it was Kamal, but he insists that both the bombings and the kidnapping plot are attempts by King Marcus to discredit him."

"Is that a possibility?"

"No. We've ruled out the Sebastianis." He paused. "If Kamal is telling the truth, then we're probably looking at terrorists. Which raises the stakes considerably. Kamal would not hurt the princess. Terrorists—"

"I get it," Hawk said, looking at Laurie, who was pretending not to listen. "You gave her the job, thinking it would be low-level danger even if they managed to kidnap her."

Laurie raised her eyes, and there was such an expression of hurt there that he immediately disliked himself for his bluntness. Still, kindness wouldn't protect her, and he grimly turned away. On the other end of the line, his father said, "She's a good agent, Son, but she's a neophyte. Take care of her."

"Yeah." He hung up.

"What's changed?"

"Someone tried to kidnap the princess. Kamal is insisting he is not responsible, and the agency thinks it might be terrorists."

"Oh." She rolled her eyes. "I've been trying to tell them that all along. I *know* it's terrorists."

"Really. How do you know?"

"I've been studying the situation for a couple of months. It's not Kamal's style to be openly aggressive. He's admittedly grief-stricken right now, and there's a lot of power hanging in the balance, but this just doesn't feel like him."

"So you took the assignment, suspecting it was terrorists you'd be fighting?"

The smallest crease appeared between her delicate eyebrows. "Yes."

"This isn't a game, you know. It's not about pretty dresses and fake fingernails."

"Well, in actuality, it is in part about dresses and fingernails. It's about being the princess, who is noted as being one of the most elegant women in the world. Her photograph appears in *Vogue* and *People*. To do her justice, I have to be as elegant as she is."

Hawk bristled feeling as if a jab of lightning had shot through his veins. "It's not about elegance. It's about staying alive."

She met his eyes head-on. "Look, once Mrs. Watson moves on, it's going to be you and me alone out there. If you don't think I can do this job, then I'm going to request your position be filled by someone who can be supportive."

"It's not that I don't think you can do it—"

"Oh, really." She smiled. "Then what is it?"

A hint of that creeping shame touched his chest. "You're just so…"

"What? Young? There are agents five years younger than me who've been on the job for a couple of years. Or maybe you meant nice. Cheerleaderish.

Maybe I need to work on being a bitch, and people would take me seriously.''

"You couldn't be a bitch if you tried."

She looked chastened at that and folded her hands together neatly on the table. "Look, I bake bread, okay? I go to church on Sundays, and I even teach a Sunday school class. I volunteer at a senior center because I like it. I was raised in a world where people are nice to each other.

"But that doesn't mean I'm stupid or naive or any of those other things you all think. I'm really smart. I understand the job. I'm trained in Tae Kwon-Do and kung fu and weapons handling. I can shoot the eye from a black-eyed pea at twenty paces and never miss. Stop stereotyping me, or else resign. I can do the job, but not without your support." She narrowed her eyes. "Are we clear?"

"Fair enough." Hawk crossed his arms. "Now *you* listen to *me*. I've lost people who thought they knew what they were doing, and I'm not going to have it happen again. Truth is, I do think you're too young and too naive for this assignment, but I also see that you're the best woman for the job on purely cosmetic reasons, and it's urgent that someone gets out there to take the princess's place."

Laurie's eyes snapped, but she was listening. He continued in a deadly calm voice. "I'm not going to resign, but you need to understand that I'm the one calling the shots here, because my job is to keep you safe. I'm your general and I expect blind obedience. Is *that* clear?"

She snapped of a crisp salute. "Sir, yes, sir."

"It's not a game, Laurie." He stood up wearily. "I don't want to see you dead at the end of it, all right?"

She bowed her head, and for one moment, he admired the swaths of chestnut the light brought out in her hair. "Yes."

"Good night," he said.

There was no reply.

Laurie did not answer him because she was close to tears, and the last thing in the world she wanted was for him to see that. Nothing like tears to demolish the tough-babe image she was trying to project. He would misunderstand the reason for her strong emotion.

The tears were not from fear or hurt, but from purest frustration. All of her life she'd been fighting to be taken seriously. She was the youngest of five children and the only girl, which had carried a double whammy. Her parents treated her like a baby long after she was past the point of needing them, and although her brothers had tortured her endlessly for liking anything remotely "girly"—like dolls or, yes, nail polish—they'd also been a wall between her and the world. They had had the best intentions, of course—to protect her from harm. But often it felt like they were protecting her from life.

The need to escape their overprotectiveness had led to her going to college out of state, to taking a job in Washington, to making nearly every decision she'd made to this point.

And now she'd finally managed to land an undercover position, one that was perfect for a new agent, and what had fate done? Stuck her with another annoying older brother who was determined to protect her from everything she wanted to taste.

Damn him! His doubts had done their work—suddenly she wasn't sure she did have what it took to do this job. Maybe there was a good reason she'd been passed over time and again.

Why had she wanted this chance so badly? Was it, as Hawk implied, the glamour of the job that appealed to her? The romance of being undercover, the excitement of donning a new identity, leaving the old one behind?

If she was honest with herself, she had to admit that part of the answer was yes. And especially in this case, where she had the opportunity to play a widely acclaimed princess, and wear evening gowns she could never afford under other circumstances, and indulge her taste for expensive shoes without a blink. Didn't every woman in America sometimes wonder how she'd look if she wore the best of everything?

But there was a lot more to it than vanity. It was also particularly satisfying to be given a shot at undercover operations on a case she'd worked so hard on during the past year. It was thrilling to know she was actually going to be working a case now, after dreaming about it for so long.

And damn it, she thought with a scowl, pushing her fingers through her hair to loosen the wet strands, she deserved the chance. The most satisfying thing of all so far had been convincing that roomful of professionals that she'd be able to pull it off.

And she could. She'd show Hawk Stone.

She'd show all of them.

The next morning, Laurie dressed in jeans, sweatshirt and tennis shoes, and pulled her hair back into a tight ponytail. Mrs. Watson was not pleased. ''We have a tremendous amount to cover today, Ms.

Lewis," she said primly over her grapefruit and black coffee. "You must hurry if we're to make our appointment with the hairdresser. It's going to take quite some time, you know."

Laurie chose a muffin from a basket of assorted breads. "You'll have to reschedule for early afternoon. There is something I have to take care of this morning."

"Oh, no, that's simply not a possibility. We have—"

"Where's Hawk?" Laurie interrupted, striding across the room to pour a glass of milk. Oh, yes, she thought, bouncing athletically in her tennis shoes, she was much stronger today.

"Hawk? Oh, James. He's just gone to dress. *He's* been up for more than an hour."

"That's great." Laurie raised a brow ironically. "Reschedule the appointment for one," she repeated. "The first appearance we have to make isn't for two days. There's plenty of time."

Without waiting for an answer, she rapped on Hawk's door. "Just a minute," he called from within. She took a bite of muffin—a most satisfying carrot-raisin monster with at least forty grams of fat, thank heavens—and turned toward the bank of long windows. The day was brilliant and sunny, green and freshly washed. The door behind her clicked open and she turned.

A wave of man-scented steam came out of the room, shaving lotion and soap with notes of pine mixed in, and it was so delicious Laurie instinctively inhaled while her mind tried to work itself around the creature standing before her in nothing but a pair of jeans that rode low on his narrow hips.

Yesterday she had noticed that he was quite a good-looking man. A woman would have to be dead or dying to miss it. His attractiveness was so complete it was nearly an exaggeration—his long, loose-limbed body, the face of a brooding angel, the hair of every Native American fantasy American women had spun for four centuries, and the voice of a rake bent on deflowering every virgin in the world.

One thing Laurie understood, however, was the male species. Four brothers and their assorted friends had removed all the mystery and mystique. No man, no matter how great looking, held any sway over Laurie Lewis unless she chose to ignore everything she knew about scratching, belching, snorting, smoking, drinking and all the rest of their bad habits. Hawk Stone had two strikes against him. The good-looking part was a big drawback. In her experience, the more handsome a guy was, the more ego he had to go with it.

And in her experience, men generally thought they were about twelve times better looking than they actually were, so one like this generally had himself cast as the headliner every time he walked into a room.

She had to admit Hawk didn't appear to use his good looks. He didn't seem vain in the slightest, nor did he employ so many of the smarmy gestures she'd grown used to in some of her brothers' good-looking friends—the little touches and long, smoldering looks, the need of such men to make sure every woman around was seeing just how fabulous he was. Hawk did none of that, and she was forced to recognize it only added to his appeal.

But the other strike against him was undeniable— that brooding aura, which Laurie just couldn't stand in anyone, male or female. She was a sensible sort and did not understand why people wasted time brooding over anything, no matter how bad. She always wanted to tell them to get on with their lives, already. She suspected Hawk was wounded in some way, that his father had dragged him into this against his will, and maybe there was a good reason for him to be so grim all the time.

That didn't mean Laurie had to like it. A good sense of humor could get you through just about anything. All brooding did was keep you in a bad place.

All that aside, Laurie was temporarily stunned by the man. His black hair was combed away from his face, and silvery water droplets dappled a supple, pale brown chest. His nipples were very dark.

"Uh…" she said.

He raised his eyebrows, evidently completely unaware of the fact that she was about to faint dead away from the sheer impact of his naked torso. "Something you want?"

Before she knew what she was doing, Laurie slid her eyes down his chest, stopping in chagrin when she got to the waistband of his jeans. Embarrassed, she looked away, glaring at the muffin in her hand. She thought about trying to eat a bite to cover her speechlessness, but she was fairly sure her mouth was too dry to do much about chewing—which gave her a good idea.

Making a little noise, she took a sip of milk and pantomimed chewing, as if she'd already had a bite in her mouth, and swallowed with exaggerated movements. She smiled. "Sorry. That was rude. I was eating."

His eyes showed nothing, and she remembered his

rudeness from the night before. Yeah, he was gorgeous, but that was no excuse for being a jerk.

"Look," she said, "I know the only reason I landed this job was because I happen to look like the princess. I also know—unlike everyone else, except maybe your father—that I have what it takes to be a good agent."

"Laurie, you don't have to—"

She held up a hand. "I'm not interested in trying to talk you into believing me. I'm going to prove it to you."

"What do you mean, prove it?"

"Get dressed and I'll show you."

"I thought you had a hair appointment or something."

"I moved it. This is more important. I'm not going to go out in the field with a partner who doesn't respect me."

Inclining his head, he fixed those cool green eyes on her and considered. "Fair enough," he said. "Let me finish dressing and we'll get out of here."

Chapter 4

Beneath the labyrinthine structure that housed the headquarters of the FBI was a warren of training areas, and it was there that Laurie took Hawk. They checked in at a heavily guarded door, where a security guard in black pants and a black turtleneck smiled at Laurie. "Hey, I heard you landed an assignment. 'Bout time." The young, blond, goateed guard nodded at Hawk. "You seen her in action yet?"

He handed over his wallet. "Not yet."

"This is Caleb Stone's son, Hawk," Laurie said. The agency had grown fond of Special Agent Stone.

"Oh, wow. Great to meet you, man."

"Thanks."

As they made their way down the hall, Laurie covered her nervousness by saying, "What's your training, Hawk? I know you were a police officer. Any martial arts? Special weapons or assignments?"

"Nothing much out of the ordinary. I'm a cop."

He shrugged. "Spent four years in the military, with tanks mainly." A faint, rueful grin lifted his mouth. "Don't suppose we'll have much need of that."

The faint amusement transformed him enough that Laurie smiled back. "Not likely, but you never know." She pushed open a door to a room filled with red mats and nodded at the instructor drilling a student there.

The latter was a burly, middle-aged man Laurie knew from several assignments, Joe Dodge. He requested her as his research expert now. "Hey, Joe," she called. She pointed Hawk to a line of chairs at one side. "You can wait there," she said, and leaned against the wall to take off her shoes.

"Laurie, babe!" Joe shook his arms. "What's up?"

"Can you take a few minutes to run me through a few drills? I'm brushing up."

"Anything for you, doll." He nodded at the instructor, who lifted a hand and left through another door. Joe twisted his neck from side to side and bounced on the balls of his feet, and Laurie hoped Hawk was catching the fact that if Joe weren't an agent, he'd be a linebacker for the NFL—six feet three inches, a powerfully muscular 245 pounds of brute strength.

She bent from the waist to stretch the back of her legs and all the muscles along her spine, then straightened and stripped off her sweatshirt, tossing it down on the mats by her discarded shoes. "Street rules," she said, and braced for his assault.

Joe's eyes glittered. "All *right*."

He lunged.

And as Laurie had known it would be, the fight

was a tough one; Joe had been one of her advocates early on, because he'd learned to respect her on the mat. He lunged now and she countered. She flipped him and he caught her foot, and then the stylistic beginning dance moves slid into a tough, scrambling, furious fight for dominance. He played to his strengths—brute size and power—and Laurie played to her own—flexibility and grace.

She also played to his weaknesses—lack of speed and short arms, and he played to hers—a lack of weight and male muscularity. Twice, he caught her. The first time, he took advantage of her being off-balance from a flip, and tucked her under one arm like a sack of groceries.

She swung her feet upward and over his shoulder, using his own leg as a vault, and took him down with a knee in his chest, but he countered with a quick roll that landed her on her back. That time, she nearly didn't escape, but managed to dive forward and roll, eluding him once again. He grabbed her by the hair and flung her to the ground, but Laurie raised a straight arm and caught him in the throat. His growl of frustration was not feigned when she rolled, tucked and blasted into his knees, careful not to really break them as she would have to in real life. His kneecap caught her high on the cheekbone, momentarily blinding her, but she had him down, at her mercy, in two seconds. Her hand was ready to tear his throat or, more likely, his tender male parts, when he cried, "Uncle!"

Laurie laughed and let him go, falling sideways to sit on the mat. Covered in sweat and breathing hard, she looked over to Hawk, who shook his head. "Princess is gonna have a black eye. That was smart."

She grinned, resting her arms over her knees. "Guess you're of the school that says if you can't say anything nasty, don't say anything at all, huh?"

For the space of a moment, she saw grudging respect in his bright green eyes, even a flicker of wry humor cross his wide, beautiful mouth. "Won't do you much good against a gun, though, will it?"

"Tough customer," Joe said with a grin. He respected toughness above all things.

"Yeah." Laurie took a breath and hauled herself to her feet, then reached down to help Joe up. Her body tingled and pulsed with confidence after her performance, and whether Hawk admitted it or not, she knew she'd shown him something here. She stopped to put her shoes on. "Damn," she said, looking at her hands. "I broke three nails."

"You'll be in big trouble with Mrs. Watson for that."

"No doubt." Laurie picked up her sweatshirt and carried it with her to the door. "Come on, tough guy," she said to Hawk. "I know a thing or two about guns, too."

Hawk followed her reluctantly, a reluctance born entirely in his abrupt notice of his partner as a female. Beneath the sweatshirt, she wore only a man-style undershirt and a sports bra with lime-colored ribbing. Sweat glistened on her chest and arms and back, stuck tendrils of hair to her face and neck. The damp cotton outlined a body that was even better than he'd been imagining, which had been pretty good—long-limbed and long-waisted, lean but not skinny. Her nipples showed through just a little bit, enough to make him wonder about the color and shape of them. There was an infinite and wonderful variety in women's nipples—something he'd forgotten these past couple of years—and it startled him to realize suddenly just how much he'd missed the pleasure of looking, touching, tasting....

Damn. She walked a little ahead of him, and her sturdy, strong movements stirred the same heat they had this morning. He liked her a lot better as a woman who could tell him to jump off a bridge, and that showed in her walk: loose and easy, strong and supple and confident.

No fear. Watching her take down a man three times her size had shown him why she had none.

"Look," he said, "you don't have to prove you can shoot. I trust you."

She stopped in the hallway, raising skeptical blue eyes to his face. "No you don't." She inclined her head and Hawk noticed the impossibly delicate line of her jaw. "And maybe I need to know where you are, too."

"Whatever," he said, annoyed again. "But I was thinking maybe you'd be happier with a good hamburger before we get back to the commandant. If we leave now, we'll have plenty of time. If we start shooting, we'll run out."

"Not yet," she said, and hauled open the door.

Hawk took a deep breath against the tension building suddenly in his chest. Downrange, another agent was practicing, and Hawk's eyelid twitched in time with the shots. The smell of fresh gunpowder burned his nostrils and he found his body drawing tight against the pictures flashing in his brain. A soft roar filled his ears, dulling the sound of Laurie checking out guns and bullets and ear coverings from a burly woman behind a counter. The woman stared at him oddly and he wondered if it showed on his face, this disgusting fear.

Numb, he followed Laurie into their booth and watched her load her gun with crisp expertise. He fitted earmuffs over his head and watched her shoot— left-handed—at a paper target with an arm that was straight and strong, with an aim that was perfect. Six bullets, four right through the heart.

He felt sweat on the back of his neck. His eyelid jerked every time she fired, and to pull himself together, he focused on her arm, that long straight arm. A nice alignment of muscles beneath skin that showed the first signs of summer tan… In contrast, a thin white scar ran from the base of her thumb up her forearm past the elbow. A very old scar, but a nasty injury once upon a time.

She stepped back, waved him forward. Hawk took a breath, aware of a trembling that did not quite show, but ran beneath his flesh from neck to groin.

A fierce, sudden steadiness came over him and he fired. Once. Twice. Thrice. His breath came harder and he fired again, feeling heat in his heart, a blaze in his head. The flickering images at the back of his mind coalesced into a single, rabid human being, lifting a gun to take with him his wife and son and a police officer who stood in his way. Bam. Bam. Bam.

The head of the target was gone. Hawk narrowed his eyes and lowered the gun.

Laurie stood to one side, her arms crossed, a measuring expression on her face. He met her gaze unapologetically, pulled off his earmuffs and said, "You ready to eat?"

"In a minute." She narrowed her eyes a little. "What's going on with the gun?"

"Long story," he said, and turned the weapon over in his hands, liking the cold, hard weight of it. "It's been a while since I shot one."

She raised one elegantly arched brow. "Looks like you haven't forgotten anything."

He put it down. "Let's go eat."

She took him to a diner not far away, a homey place that was an anomaly in the glitzy neighborhood. Hawk liked it immediately—the plate-glass window with Jerry's Diner painted in an arch over Best Pies in the World; the plump, middle-aged waitress who took their order; the red Naugahyde booth and Formica tabletops. "This is okay!" he said approvingly.

"I like it, too," Laurie said, flipping through the charts in the tabletop juke box. "There's one just like it in my hometown. What's your pleasure in music?" She inclined her head. "I'm betting you're a rock 'n' roll kinda guy."

He lifted one eyebrow. "Maybe."

She grinned, the expression quick and impish. In her sweatshirt and ponytail, she looked like a tomboy who'd just come in from feeding the horses. "I'm right, admit it." She dug some coins out of her pocket and put them in the machine. "You probably like all those whiney Springsteen types."

Hawk couldn't help it; he chuckled, then leaned forward. "And you're into happy little love songs. Singalong songs."

"Wrong-o, buddy. Give me some hard guitar every time, the louder, the better."

"Really?"

She grinned. "No. My brothers liked it like that. Give me waltzes and Karen Carpenter. But I guessed right on your tastes, didn't I?"

"'Fraid so. I hate being so predictable."

"Oh, other than that, you're quite mysterious." Her nostrils quivered and he realized he was being teased.

He gave a mock sigh, leaned back and relaxed. "Thank God. A guy's gotta have some mystery."

Their drinks came—iced tea for both. Laurie added a copious amount of sugar to hers and said, "So, partner, why don't you tell me a little about yourself? We're stuck together for the next two weeks, after all. Might as well know a little about each other."

Hawk drank his tea straight, and took a long cooling sip of it. Excellent. "What d'you want to know?"

"You're a cop, right? So what are you doing here instead of working the beat?"

He lifted one shoulder. "My dad asked me for a favor. He wanted you for this job, but he also wanted someone to act as bodyguard."

"Yeah? So why you? Why not pick one of a dozen other bodyguard types around the FBI? It's not like we have a shortage."

For a moment, Hawk said nothing. He peered into his glass, looking at the cubes of ice in their swimming pool of tea, then raised his head. "I quit the force about two months ago. My partner was killed in January and I guess I just…" He let go of a breath, finding it strange to say it out loud to someone he didn't know. "I've had a hard time getting over it."

"I'm sorry," she said. "Do you want to talk about it?"

"No." He smiled to take the abruptness out of his

response. "Just one of those things. Happens a dozen times a day, all over the country."

She nodded gently. "It explains your concern, though. Thank you for telling me." Leaning forward, she added, "Are you reassured that I know what I'm doing?"

"Yes. I trust you not to get yourself killed. Still, I'm the boss on security measures, all right?"

"Absolutely, Captain." She saluted with her left hand, and he spied the long thin scar on her arm again.

"Where did you get the scar?" he asked.

She laid her arm flat on the table and pulled up her sweatshirt to reveal the length of it. This close, Hawk could see the tiny holes where stitches had once held the skin together. "My badge of honor," she said with a grin. "None of my brothers has a scar anywhere near as good as this."

"Your brothers sound like hellions."

"That's understating the case by quite a bit," she said and ran her finger up the scar in an unselfconscious and somehow sexy gesture. "I broke my arm in five places—took three hours of surgery to put it all back together again, and I never cried once."

"How did you do it?"

She gave a quick shrug. "Fell out of the loft in the barn."

"Ow."

Their hamburgers came, and they leaned back to let the waitress put them down—steaming, giant burgers with all the trimmings. "I was seriously starving last night," Laurie said, slathering mustard on her bun. "I'll be so glad to get rid of the commandant."

"It was a good burger, too."

"And you didn't even save me a bite like you agreed to."

"I will in the future, I promise."

Cutting the burger in half neatly, she picked up one portion. "So, you're obviously Native American, and your father is not, so your mother must be, right? Where did you grow up?"

Hawk took off the lettuce and tomatoes, but left the onions when he saw that Laurie had. They could breathe horrible fumes over Mrs. Watson together. "I'm *Indian*," he said with subtle emphasis. "My mother was Dineh—what you call Navajo—and I grew up in Flagstaff, and on the rez itself. Hand me that ketchup, please."

"So what's that like? The reservation?"

He took the bottle and shook out a pool onto his plate for his fries. "Quiet. Poor. Pretty peaceful. I still have land out there—that's where I keep the horses."

"But you live in town now?"

"Yeah. Too far to get to work."

She nodded, busy with her hamburger. Hawk ate, too, surprised that it was okay to just sit and be quiet with this woman. "I miss having animals around," she said. "Growing up, we had everything."

"What did you have?"

"Oh, you name it—the cows, of course, and horses. Dogs and cats and rabbits and ferrets and rats and oh, everything. We all had our special little love affair with some weird animal."

"What was yours?"

"Let's see—mainly the cats, you know, but I raised rabbits for a while for 4-H. Won prizes for my lops—rabbits—too, by the way. I hated having to sell them, though, so I quit. I had a lizard for a while, too, but he wasn't very affectionate, so I gave him to my brother Lincoln.''

"You don't really have a brother named Lincoln. Do you?''

She grinned. "Lincoln, Garfield, Kennedy and King. For Martin Luther King—he was born three days after the assassination.'' She touched her chest. "And Laurie, for my aunt, who died of cancer just before I was born.''

Hawk inclined his head, oddly touched. "No offense, but you wouldn't think somebody from the Heartland would have put that much stock in a man a lot of people saw as a rabble-rouser.''

"You have to stop that,'' she said, raising her eyebrows. "Equating Midwest with backward.''

"I probably am, but sometimes a stereotype has elements of truth.''

"No,'' she said, shaking her head with a smile. "It's conservative in a way, but everything is based on true decency, a spirit of love your neighbor, all that. My parents thought the world of Martin Luther King because he was a good, Christian man and practiced nonviolence. My dad says my mother cried all day when she found out he was shot.''

"My apologies,'' he said.

"It's all right.'' Laurie wiped her hands with a sigh. "How is it that I keep asking questions about you and then we keep talking about me?''

"I'm good, that's why.''

"Come on, Mr. Mysterious. Spill all. Do you have sisters and brothers?''

"No, cousins. My mom died when I was pretty young and my dad was always traveling with the

army, so I lived with my aunt and uncle and their
kids—two girls and a boy, all younger than me.''

"I bet they aren't named for presidents.''

"No. Anna, Jeremy and Mark.'' He glanced at the
clock and straightened abruptly. "Hell, it's twelve-
thirty.''

"Yikes! I'm going to be in big trouble if I'm late.
I'm sure I'm seeing someone name Geoffrey with a
G who doesn't take kindly to being kept waiting.''
She looked at her watch, scowled and said, "Maybe
I ought to call the commandant and tell her I'll meet
her wherever we're going. You'll be all right getting
back by yourself, won't you?'' Already out of the
booth, Laurie stopped to pull bills from her pocket,
and Hawk couldn't help noticing the length of her
legs again. "I mean, new city and all that, not that
you're—''

"I understood. I'll be fine. Go call her.''

Laurie rushed off, her ponytail bouncing. Hawk noticed three guys at the counter all turn to apprecia-
tively watch the swing of her hips. He remembered
how she looked in one of the evening gowns, low cut,
tight, and thought with a sense of satisfaction that the
poor suckers just had no idea.

He watched her at the telephone, talking rapidly,
nodding, explaining, and it occurred to him that
maybe his father was right—he'd needed this assignment. There was something refreshing about Laurie
Lewis, like a clean wind blowing away all the heavy
air.

Interesting.

She hurried back toward him and her breasts
bounced a little, a sight he and all the guys at the
counter appreciated in equal measure. For a long sec-

ond, Hawk wanted to be the guy she was coming to kiss goodbye before she rushed out, the one they'd all envy. He stood as she approached the table.

"She's annoyed," Laurie said. "I'll be on bread and water tonight, you'll see—so it's good that you fed me."

"I'll order a steak for dinner, the biggest on the menu, and smuggle it into your room if I have to."

She grinned. "Thanks. And thanks for going with me." She stuck out her hand. "Partners?"

He accepted the offering, glad of the chance to touch her. But something strange happened as their palms met—a weird bolt of sensation that made everything seem to switch into slow motion. Their fingers did not behave, but twisted together, sliding, exploring, touching. Telling himself he was doing it to score points with the guys at the counter, Hawk impulsively lifted her hand to his lips. "Sure, partner," he said, meeting her eyes above her fingers.

In the blue irises he saw surprise and dismay as his lips lightly brushed her knuckles. But it was worse for Hawk, because he realized he was flirting with her. Flirting with her because he liked her. Flirting because she'd kindled desire in him, desire that felt suspiciously as if it might kick-start the deadened parts of him.

And she was way too nice to be used that way. He'd have to be the biggest jerk on the planet to mess with Laurie Lewis's honest, loving heart.

He winked broadly. "Think I scored some points with the guys at the counter with that?"

She looked a little unsettled, but then got the joke and grinned, her eyes crinkling impishly. "Definitely.'' She took back her hand. ''See you in a little while. I'll be dead gorgeous by then, so prepare yourself.''

''I'll do my best.''

Chapter 5

The stylist's name was not Geoffrey, but Juanito. He was a tiny Puerto Rican with enormous, beautiful eyes, who sighed sadly when Laurie arrived in her sweaty ponytail. "This one?" he said with hopelessness to Mrs. Watson.

"Yes. Do your best. Color and cut as we discussed. Probably a facial as well."

"Oh, yes. Yes. That's important." He directed Laurie to a chair in the empty salon and touched her face. "What is your usual routine, Ms. Lewis?"

"Soap and water."

"You're lucky to have such naturally beautiful skin, but it will not last, you know, unless we get you taking care of it properly. I think we'll go with oatmeal for exfoliation, then avocado to restore the moisture balance. What do you think?"

She grinned at him in the mirror. "You're the boss."

It was not an unpleasant afternoon, especially when Juanito proved to be funny, irreverent and absolutely wonderful at his chosen profession. His hands were gentle and firm by turns as he massaged her face and scalp. He threw in a neck rub for nothing, turning Laurie into a blob of human female completely at his disposal. He cut and plucked and colored, and it wasn't until Laurie was under the cloak of the dryer that she thought again about Hawk.

Or rather, Hawk's mouth on her hand. The effect of his voice on her spine. His eyes—distant and sad, intimate and hungry all at once—on her face. Her lips. Her breasts. Her legs. He looked at her a lot, discreetly, and not in a rude way, but with a gratifyingly absorbed kind of interest.

It was a bit of a new experience for her. Oh, it wasn't that she hadn't had boyfriends. She had—a couple of them serious enough that they'd even gone to a sexual relationship—and she knew what it was like to be desired.

But mostly, men noticed Laurie for other reasons. She didn't draw the smoldering types. She drew the nice ones, the daddy types, the ones hungry to settle down. Responsible men. Honest men. Men who kissed tenderly and made love respectfully and gratefully.

Hawk smoldered and brooded. He was a simmering cauldron of all sorts of conflicting emotions. He would not kiss politely or make love gently.

And it was entirely inappropriate to be having such thoughts about her partner. It was against all the rules of the job. She should treat him like anyone else.

How was she going to do that with his eyes dancing all over her, though?

"Oh, no, no. Don't frown so," cried Juanito, lifting the dryer. "What could be such a problem?" Taking her hand gallantly, he helped her up. "Must be a man. It's always a man. Come over here and let me comb you out while you tell me all about him."

Her hair was set on enormous rollers—"Do you see how that gives your hair a simple, smooth bounce?"—and he started taking them out, pointing out one thing and another about caring for the new style, as he solicited information about her love life. "What's the trouble with this guy?" he asked.

"There really isn't any trouble," Laurie said. "He's just very attractive and I have to work with him—alone for two weeks. I'd like to keep things under control."

"How attractive?"

"Very. Sexy," she found herself adding.

"Oooh. So what's the problem? If you think you aren't going to catch his eye, trust me, he'll fall over when he sees you like this." He fluffed her hair a little and squinted suddenly at her reflection in the mirror. "Oh, my stars. You look so much like that princess...what's her name?" He put the brush down, rushed over to a stack of glossy gossip magazines and flipped through them until he found a particular issue. "Oh, this is too good, honey." He held up a photograph of Princess Julia, snapped by paparazzi with a long lens, obviously. Looking faintly unhappy, the princess was staring out a window. "You're *her!*"

A teeny bit alarmed at what he might put together, Laurie took the magazine and looked at the photograph closely. "You're sweet, Juanito, but this woman is so amazing."

"No, no, no, no. Look at her. Look at yourself.

You want that guy? There's not a man in this country who isn't lusting over this princess. Give him his fantasy, honey. You'll do fine.''

Laurie laughed. If only he knew. ''Thanks, Juanito.''

She was a bit weary by the time Mrs. Watson put her through yet more diplomatic paces at the hotel. Hawk, thankfully, wasn't there to observe. Mrs. Watson had drilled him earlier, and Laurie suspected he'd escaped the commandant out of self-preservation. All Laurie wanted was a nice hot bath and a good night's sleep, but after ordering a meal of broiled chicken breasts and freshly grilled vegetables, which Laurie had to admit were delicious, and having a manicurist in to fix her broken nails, the older woman had yet one more task for her to perform.

A dress rehearsal.

''You're ready for the charity events,'' Mrs. Watson said, ''where you'll be carefully escorted and no one will come close, but I'm concerned about the more intimate dinners.'' She marched into the bedroom and flung open the closet doors. ''What would you like to wear?'' She smiled, for the first time seeming like a kindly aunt instead of a drill sergeant.

Laurie smiled in return, letting her pleasure show as she ran her hands over the rainbow of glorious designer gowns. She took out a simple red silk that looked like nothing on the hanger, but had been astonishing when she put it on in the dressing room. ''This one,'' she said.

''Excellent. Now, put yourself in the princess's mind and choose your jewels for the evening.'' Mrs.

Watson put a case on the bed and opened it, revealing a glittering, gorgeous display of jewels.

"Oh, my!" Laurie gazed at them in wonder. "They aren't real?"

"Oh, no. Not even the princess wears real jewels unless the occasion is very special indeed. These are all paste, but as you see, they're very good quality." She stepped back. "What would like to wear tonight, your highness?"

Laurie looked at her, uncertain, then realized this was where it began. She had to forget about herself, about the long struggle to get to this job, about Hawk, even about what judgments Mrs. Watson would make. Starting tonight, she had to think like the princess, walk like the princess, talk like the princess.

Drawing in a breath, she let herself fill with the sense of elegance and quiet and dignity that surrounded Julia like a rare perfume. The dress was quite dramatic, so any jewelry would tone it down. She took out a single ruby dangling on a fine chain and a pair of equally delicate earrings. "These should do," she said in the princess's cultured tones. "And the red shoes, please."

Mrs. Watson scurried forward. "Of course, your highness. I'll be glad to do your hair as well, unless you'd prefer to leave it down."

"Not for such a formal evening. A simple twist, I think."

Mrs. Watson smiled in approval. "Very nice, Laurie. Now get dressed and we'll run through a few scenarios, all right?"

Laurie beamed. "Of course."

Hawk had needed a breather by the time he escaped the hotel room. He was unsettled by his attraction to

long-legged Laurie, but he'd also been dismayed by
his reaction at the gun range. Had he lost his nerve?

Since he'd never been there, he decided to head for
the Wall, joining hundreds of other tourists as they
visited monuments and memorials of all kinds. He
bought a hot dog from a sidewalk vendor and ate it
as he walked, thinking he'd seen these views so often
on television that they almost didn't seem real.

The sun was starting to hang low on the horizon
by the time he made it to the Vietnam Memorial.
He'd deliberately saved it for last, unsure how he felt
about it, about the war that had taken his father away
from his mother and into another world entirely.

The crowds had thinned as he approached, giving
him a clear view of the landmark he'd seen often in
pictures and on television. But unlike the Washington
Memorial, sticking like a big white finger into the
sky, the impact of the Wall was much more subtle. It
seduced him to walk down the gentle slope, the names
sparse to begin with, the lists growing longer and
longer as he reached the middle. He walked by people
making rubbings of one name or another, past tiny
vases with single flowers. A teddy bear nestled at the
bottom of one panel, obviously new, and the sight of
it made his throat catch. He walked on.

At the center, he paused and stepped back a little
way to see if he could take it in. Overhead, the sky
was a deep rose, a vivid contrast to the shiny, black
granite wall, and on either side of the V, the names
stretched for a block. Hawk thought of his father, and
the idea that his name might have ended up carved
into that granite suddenly made his heart ache.

For the first time in his life, he really thought about

Caleb Stone fighting in that lonely jungle so far away. He'd been drafted at eighteen. Eighteen! It seemed so painfully young now to Hawk. What did anyone know at eighteen? What could that have been like?

And then, to have the entire country in an uproar about it, so angry and divided... For a long time, Hawk had been angry with his father for wandering the world instead of coming home. But standing there in the still evening, seeing those names, Hawk thought maybe he understood it for the first time. Caleb Stone, being the man he was, would have found it impossible to return to the life he'd known.

Slowly, Hawk walked up the other side, this time taking time to stop and read the names. Not all of them. But at each panel, he stopped and read a few of the names of the boys and men who had not returned from that lonely jungle war so far away. It seemed the least he could do—to think of them for a few seconds, each of them.

At the other side, he started to walk away, and found a thick lump in his throat. He stopped and looked back.

A grizzled man who looked like a biker said, "Gets to you, don't it?"

"Yeah," he said. "It really does."

Still a little unsettled, a little lost in time, Hawk let himself into the hotel room a half hour later. He heard voices—Mrs. Watson and Laurie, but Laurie-as-Julia, and he smiled to himself as he came around the corner into the sitting room.

And stopped dead. Standing in the middle of the room, in a red dress that showed every swoop and curve of her body, was Laurie, looking exactly like the princess. Her hair was swept up into some tony knot. A red jewel dangled at the hollow of her throat, and between that jewel and the top of the dress was a greater expanse of the most perfect skin he'd ever seen. It almost glowed.

Seeing him, she smiled, giving her eyes an impish little light. In the princess's voice, she said, "Hello, Hawk. Please join us, won't you?"

"Wow," he said respectfully.

"Like it?" She turned in a circle, her arms outstretched.

"Oh, yeah." It was the kind of dress that made a man wonder what in the world could be holding it up and what, if anything, was beneath it. The top seemed to barely be clinging to the swell of her breasts, which he thought were moving a little too freely to be bound by much. The skirt cupped her bottom and outlined her endless legs.

And yet the dress was also perfectly decent. The neckline was not too low. The cut somehow hid as much as it revealed. It was just that airy, scarflike business that made a man hope something might come along to blow it right off those peekaboo curves.

He realized his ears were hot and he was staring like a love-struck dog. "Just be sure you have a place to put your gun," he growled. "I'm going to bed." He nodded curtly at them. "Good night."

Laurie watched him retreat with her hands on her hips. "Oh, here we go again," she said. "Mrs. Watson, will you excuse me a minute?"

"Certainly, my dear. Honestly, I believe I'm all in, anyway. I'm going to tuck myself in with a nice cup of tea. We're done—you're going to do a wonderful job. If you need anything at all, don't hesitate to call."

Impulsively, Laurie bent down to kiss her cheek. "Thank you, Mrs. Watson. I couldn't have done it without you."

The older woman patted her arm, then inclined her head. "Go set him straight, Princess."

Laurie started across the room in her usual stride, then remembered to slow down and gracefully *glide* over the carpet in her very high heels. She liked the powerful feeling three-inch heels added to her already substantial height—made her nearly six feet tall.

Right on eye level with Hawk, who opened the door at her knock and stood there cloaked in his brooding hostility. "What?" he said.

"I thought we went through this already," she stated, crossing her arms.

"Went through what?"

"The whole brooding thing."

"Yeah, and I thought we got through the shallow thing."

"And you were supposed to quit being a snot."

He tried to hang on to the growly look, but couldn't. "Snot?" he said. "What're we, ten?"

"If the shoe fits."

He took a breath and met her eyes squarely. "I was escaping the dress, sweetheart." He licked his bottom lip. "I'm still trying not to look at it."

Oh, heavens, he had the best voice. When he lowered it so suggestively, it sent shivers down her spine. "Really?" she countered softly.

She saw him swallow at that, and her heart started beating just a little faster at the feeling in the room.

She was suddenly aware of the great amounts of skin that showed. Was aware of the swell of her breasts and the length of her arms, aware of every centimeter of flesh brushed by air that suddenly seemed very cool.

"Yeah," he said, and if he had been a tiger, his tail would have switched. The green of his eyes was very bright in their frame of dark lashes. "Really."

And the part of her that was tired of safe men, simple men, suddenly wanted to know what it would be like to tease a tiger, just a little. "I've never had a chance to wear a dress like this. What does a man think when he sees a woman wearing one?"

His nostrils flared and he stepped back one pace, crossing his arms over his chest, his legs slightly spread. An aggressive stance to go with the bold look he licked her with—and she felt it tangibly, that gaze, sweeping her shoulders, lingering obviously on her breasts, caressing her waist and legs. "He thinks how little you must be wearing underneath it," he said quietly, raising his eyes to her face. "And what you're thinking to make your nipples so hard."

"You know what?" Laurie said, flushing painfully. "You're a lot worse than a snot. That was uncalled for."

She whirled, irritated at herself for wanting his good opinion, and at him for being so obnoxious. "Good night, Mr. Stone," she snapped.

But as she was about to slam the door, he caught her by the upper arm. "Wait." She tried to pull free, but he held her firmly. "Please."

She didn't look at him, kept her head turned away. He didn't let her go immediately, and she was aware of his touch even when it infuriated her that she could want a man who could say something so crude. The dress that had given her so much pleasure now seemed tawdry and slutty, and she was embarrassed that she'd been thinking she looked lusciously elegant.

"Laurie," he said in that woodsy, smoky voice, very close to her ear. "Will you please look at me?" One hand pushed hair away from her eyes and she ducked away from it.

"Just say what you need to say and let me go to bed."

"Yeah, well, it would be easier if you'd look at me."

She breathed in, acutely aware now of the way her breasts were exposed, of the fact that her nipples probably did show. She was going to have to do something about that—but it wasn't like she didn't have a bra on. She did. Maybe something heavier...

"Laurie," he said patiently, still holding her upper arm.

She rolled her eyes and looked at him. "What?"

He was close. Much closer than he'd ever been before, and she smelled the faint saltiness of his skin, the lingering scent of sage on his hair. "That was bad. Really bad, and I'm sorry. Truth is, you've had me a little bit worked up all day, and what I'd really like is to get rid of all this fabric and just have a good athletic romp to burn off some tension."

Laurie swallowed, wondering if she had the courage to accept that offer.

"But," he continued, his eyes going dark as they slipped down her body, "we have work to do, and sex just complicates everything, and..." He let go of a breath. "Hell. You look so good in that."

She was conscious of a ripple of something moving
down her neck from her hairline, giving her goose
bumps. Defensively, she crossed her arms again.

Hawk gave her a half smile, looking down quickly,
then back to her face. "That's not helping all that
much."

"Cleavage," she said, looking down at herself.
"Never knew it was possible."

"God, Laurie," he growled. "Just go, will you?"

She laughed. "Gotcha!" she said, and turned away.
But he didn't let her go. Suddenly, his grip was fierce
and he put his other hand on her stomach and pushed
her against the door, holding her there with his body.

"This isn't a game," he said, his breath touching
her mouth. "There are a lot of men out there who
aren't going to give a damn if you're a princess or a
whore, they'll take whatever they want, however they
can get it. Those terrorists aren't a bunch of polite
gentlemen who'll put you up in a nice suite and protect your virtue."

His mouth was barely two inches away—a wide,
strong mouth with an upper lip carved as sharply as
obsidian, the lower one much fuller and more seductive. His face was so close she could see individual
eyelashes. And very distinctly, against her belly, she
felt his erection.

She was very aroused by him, by the danger of the
situation, by his anger, and with a recklessness she
had never dreamed she had, she raised her eyes. "I
guess it will be the dress that turns them into animals,
huh?"

For harsh seconds he stared back at her, furious and
hungry, and she thought he might let his emotions get
the better of him. That he might kiss her with that

blaze on his lips and she would taste the darkness on his tongue, the anger and despair she felt lurking. His breath was uneven, as was hers. Their chests brushed with each uneven breath, somehow more erotic than if they were pressed hard together.

Around them was utter silence, filled only with the push of air through the vents and the roar of the chemistry between them. His gaze burned her lips and his hand stretched on her belly, his fingers moving infinitesimally....

Abruptly, he pushed himself away. "We don't want to do this." He walked away, turning his back on her. "You'd better go."

Laurie left.

Chapter 6

By morning, Laurie wondered what in the world had gotten into her. She was furious with herself for her unprofessional behavior, and she was embarrassed at acting so much out of character. She ate breakfast in her room, packing as she sipped tea and nibbled on a croissant and tried to puzzle out the reasons for her actions last night. Was she trying to figure out how to be a tough-babe agent?

Maybe it was true that the women who had advanced ahead of her in the field were tougher or faster, and it was certainly true that she wanted what they had, but was that the way to get it? Did she really want to give up who she was?

And really, what was so great about Hawk Stone, anyway? She rolled her eyes. He would offer excitement, but she'd never, ever longed to experience the up-and-down adrenaline rushes mixed with emotional crashes that came with it. There would be a few weeks, maybe a few months, of giddy effervescence while she basked in his attention and worried over his moods, and then what?

A lifetime of more of the same? Ugh.

No, the reliable accountant types, those tender and thoughtful guys, might be less exciting, but how long did the excitement last, anyway? Those men would be there on Saturday mornings, mowing the grass, taking the kids to the zoo, remembering after supper to ask her about her day. A man like Hawk Stone would be good for thrills, but not much else in the long run.

With a toss of her head, Laurie renewed her resolve to forget about his gorgeous self and focus on doing a great job here. Even that was being undermined by her attraction to Hawk, and she really couldn't allow that to happen.

When she went into the bathroom to get ready, she saw that she did indeed sport a black eye this morning. It wasn't terrible and should fade in a day or two, but she had to apply her makeup carefully to conceal it. The minute she stepped out in the world as Princess Julia Sebastiani, the paparazzi were sure to show up in droves.

Face finished, she dressed carefully in a champagne linen suit, a pencil-slim skirt and fitted jacket that accented her curves very nicely. In the dressing room, Laurie had been amazed at the transformation of her body from something strong and lean to this collection of curves, and she decided again that she liked it. A lot. She'd never thought of herself as curvy, but she guessed she'd just been hiding her attributes, because there they were.

She added silk stockings, two-toned Italian heels

and the final touch—a gold-and-diamond bracelet with Greek symbols, a copy of the princess's signature piece. As she fixed the latch on her wrist Laurie wondered why Julia wore it so consistently. Had it been a present for a special occasion? A gift from a beloved relative—or a lover?

When she was finished, she stood in front of the floor-length mirror to examine herself critically—but even she, with all her doubts, saw that the transformation was just this side of astonishing. Her hair was several shades darker than it had been yesterday, and she'd swept it into the princess's trademark French twist, a style of timeless elegance. At her earlobes were small gold buttons. There was something not quite right, something missing, and she stared at herself, trying to figure out what it might be.

The answer was so obvious, she chuckled. Lipstick. She needed a slightly darker shade, and she went to the bathroom to collect her cosmetic bag and switch lipsticks. Laurie's taste ran to corals, but the princess definitely favored berry shades—and when Laurie applied it, she saw why. So much better for their coloring! She blotted her lips, dropped the lipstick in her purse and picked up the blush compact she'd put on the sink.

A knock sounded at her bedroom door and Laurie started, dropping her blush into the sink, where the powder cake shattered into a thousand pieces. "Shoot," she said, scowling. "Just a minute!" Staring at the bits and pieces of rose powder all over the marble bowl, she bit her lip. Hawk was on the other side of that door. She had to look in his face now, after…after…

Oh, good grief! How did other women do that? Act

so silly and seductive? She could just imagine the hoots and snorts of her brothers over her behavior. It was so ridiculously not her. Growling softly under her breath, she went to the door and yanked it open.

And of course, it was Hawk, dressed in a crisp black suit and tie, his hair loose and shining on his shoulders. The loose hair, paired with the suit, made him look mysteriously delectable, and in spite of her resolve, Laurie felt a helpless rush of heat move through her body. His brown throat, visible at the opening of his shirt, caught her eye and she focused there. Safer than his eyes. "I'm almost ready," she said, pretending she didn't know what he was going to say.

"Mrs. Watson went down to arrange for some food to take with us," he said. "I thought we oughta clear the air before she gets back."

His husky voice, so quiet and rich, was like a hand on some secret erotic center, and Laurie hated herself for the way her body responded. In the back of her mind, she heard her brothers hooting in derision, just as they had when any of them figured out she had a crush on one of their friends, and embarrassment made her harsh.

Her head snapped up. "As far as I'm concerned, there's nothing to talk about."

"That's not the way to play this, Laurie." He sounded patient, like an older brother. "I was a jerk last night, and I'm sorry."

"Well, so was I. Playing with fire and all that." She sighed, noticed there were tiny bits of blush sticking to her fingers, and brushed them together carefully to avoid soiling her clothes. "No harm, no foul, right?"

"We're going to be together twenty-four hours a day for the next two weeks. It might not be a bad idea to establish some ground rules."

"Fine."

The slightest smile lifted one side of his mouth. "You're really pissed, aren't you?"

Laurie crossed her arms, bowed her head, admitted it. "Not at you. At myself, for being such an idiot."

He said nothing for a long moment, and while she waited, Laurie stared at the toes of his shoes, aware that she was really an ordinary, boring kind of woman in spite of this chance to be the princess. Take away the gowns, the jewels, the accent and all you had was a girl from Nebraska who took meals to shut-ins. Boring!

"Hey," he said quietly. When she didn't look up, he put two fingers under her chin and raised her head himself. "In case you hadn't noticed, it was me in there wanting you so bad it made my hands shake." He took a step closer, let the hand on her face cup her cheek. "I'm still wanting, right now, to kiss you. How does that make *you* an idiot?"

She put up her hand in defense. "If you kiss me now, you're going to ruin my makeup."

For a moment, it seemed he didn't understand. Then his eyes hardened and he shook his head, stepping back. "Forget it. We're partners. That's plenty."

"Excellent," she said as Julia. "My bags are ready. Shall we call for the bellboy?"

He looked at her for a long moment. "Sure, princess. I'll get right on it."

Press releases had been timed to hit the tabloid offices by ten that morning, but Laurie was a little dismayed to discover the press corps already on the street outside the hotel. She halted in the lobby, seeing through the glass doors a pair of photographers talking, drinking coffee out of paper cups. A limousine waited at the curb, complete with a suited driver in dark glasses who was so obviously FBI Laurie wanted to giggle. But then, what did she know of celebrity drivers? Maybe they all looked like this.

Which was all just a very nervous reaction to realizing it was showtime. Her stomach flipped and she suddenly reached in her purse for a pair of elegant dark glasses.

"Good touch," Hawk said at her elbow, and moved ahead to open the door. Laurie took a deep breath and became the princess, moving liquidly over the rich carpet of the lobby in her expensive heels, remembering to keep her head high. She called up the princess's smile, letting it flicker over her mouth as she stepped out of the lobby into the sunlight. She waved, as the princess often did, but did not speak, trusting Hawk to provide blocking, which he did most effectively.

They ducked into the limousine amid whirring cameras and a volley of inane questions. "Hey, Princess, are you glad to be back in America?"

"Are you ready to talk about Luigi?"

"Can you comment on your brother's disappearance?"

"Do you think he's still alive?"

It was over remarkably quickly, then they were tucked into the elegant car, enveloped in silence and reflective glass. Laurie smoothed her skirt and frowned out the window. "Those are cruel questions.

Her brother has only been missing for a few months. She has to be hurting and worried.''

Hawk snorted. ''Media people are so well known for their sensitivity, after all.''

Still, Laurie frowned. ''I wonder what happened to her marriage. What made her retreat like that?''

''I'm not a big follower of celebrity gossip.''

''That's true.'' She took off the glasses. ''Whew. That was a lot more terrifying than I expected.''

''You looked perfect. I promise.''

''Thank you.''

Laurie didn't know what she'd been expecting to happen at the airport—maybe the ordinary experience of boarding a plane like anybody else, possibly without the hassle of tickets. But that wasn't how it happened at all. The limo bypassed the main airport terminals and looped around to an open area where a plane waited. It looked like an ordinary jet except for the paint job, which was a little more elegant in some way she couldn't quite pinpoint. A set of stairs led to the body of the plane, and on either side of the steps waited a retinue of uniformed staff.

All men, Laurie noticed, frowning a little.

The wind blew, warm but gusty, as they stepped out of the car, and Laurie put her hand to her hair to make sure it didn't get too tousled, suddenly understanding the need for hats and scarves. It was a strange thing to worry about—the state of her hairdo— and she couldn't think of a single other time in her life that she'd cared about the wind messing up her hair. But she had to admit to a little concern over her appearance as she and Hawk were led to the plane. Another little knot of reporters and photographers huddled at the fence stretched across the blacktop near the plane. Hawk put his hand proprietarily on the small of her back, blocking her from view.

The uniformed men greeted her obsequiously. A gray-haired man with the large dark eyes of Omar Shariff introduced himself as the pilot, Captain Joseph Corsentino. His accent was entirely American, but anyone looking on would think him a native of Montebello, along with the others, all obviously agents hired for this job. "We'll wait until we're inside to introduce everyone," the captain said, bowing over her hand in a show of deference, "but let's make it look good for the reporters."

"Of course." Without thinking, Laurie answered as the princess. "Best all around."

Conscious of the photographers, she imagined balancing a book on her head as she climbed the steps— and had one bad moment when her heel caught on an edge of a step and she nearly walked out of it.

Hawk caught her elbow, giving her a moment to recapture the pump, and she leaned over as if she was communicating some bit of information to her bodyguard. "Thanks."

"Anytime."

She had to blink at the transition to the interior of the plane, and then stopped dead. "Oh, my God!" she whispered with a little laugh, and turned around to Hawk. Not wanting to look any more like a hick from Nebraska than she already did, she only widened her eyes to express her amazement at the luxury in which they suddenly found themselves.

It was like a narrow living room. Cherry-wood panels lined the walls, exquisitely carved in a bead pattern at the edges. A Persian carpet in hues of blue and rose covered the floor. Elegant cherry tables, cleverly designed to safeguard drinks and plates they might hold, clustered close to a sofa and two over-stuffed chairs. "Good morning," said a steward in chef's whites. A swarthy, cheerful looking man with curly dark hair and a warm smile, he had the accent of a native Montebellan—the hints of Italian and British musically mixed. "I am Francesco, and I have been cooking for Princess Julia for more than a decade. It gives me great pleasure to serve you in her absence. May I show you the features of our delightful airplane?"

Charmed, Laurie smiled. "Ae-ro-plane," he'd said. "Please."

He gestured. "This is the sitting room, of course. And through this doorway, we have the bedroom and bath." Laurie and Hawk followed him into a room as tastefully decorated as the first, with a double bed tucked into one corner, a chair in another, and a solid-looking door that swung into a tiny bathroom, luxuriously appointed with gold-and-black marble.

Hawk whistled. "Wow!"

"We'll be cleared for takeoff shortly, and I will be in to serve snacks when we've attained our cruising altitude," Francesco said. "Our galley is toward the front of the plane, so allow me to settle you into your seats and make you comfortable. Shall we?"

Laurie grinned at Hawk as they followed the steward back to the living area. Hawk winked. "I guess the rich really are different, huh?"

"I would say so."

They settled in their seats and belted in. Francesco brought them drinks—coffee for Hawk, iced tea for Laurie. Francesco tsked. "You must never drink iced tea in public. The princess does not care for it. Hot or not at all.''

''All right. What shall I choose then?''

''I will be happy to serve you iced tea this afternoon, but the princess prefers an Italian soda, peach, or plain soda with lime.''

''Excellent, Francesco. Thank you.''

The trip to Chicago was not a long one, and Laurie spent the time reviewing the printed materials she had on the princess. She wished desperately that she'd thought to ask for the videotapes she'd been reviewing in the hotel, along with some others she had at work—because there was a VCR, DVD player, stereo and television screen built into the wall of the plane.

It was an array of toys no man could resist, and Hawk was no exception. He spent most of the trip playing with one or another of them. ''Look at this,'' he said more than once, and showed her the trick of the moment. Laurie, concentrating on the public appearance she would be required to put on this afternoon, only nodded distractedly.

She was scared to death, suddenly aware of all that she didn't know about the princess—a fact illuminated by the detail of the iced tea.

The whole process was like that. She got to the point where she'd figured most of it out, and some small detail would rise up to taunt her. What was her favorite color? What did she do when she couldn't sleep at night?

But none of those things mattered just now. The event in Chicago was not difficult—she had to speak for ten minutes at a celebratory opening of a child care center for immigrant children, then use giant scissors to cut a red ribbon. It would no doubt be

crowded with photographers, but as the first appearance of the princess, it would give Laurie a chance
to rehearse publicly without spending so much time
there she'd be likely to blow it.

From a file, she withdrew an enormous stack of
photographs of the princess, most of them taken before her seclusion two years ago. Laurie had organized them chronologically, the earliest taken when
Julia was about seventeen. They showed a laughing
young woman, sure of her place and her beauty, completely comfortable in the role of a royal, but smart
enough to realize there was more to life. There were
several of her at tennis matches, at balls, at charity
events and royal outings. A lot of photographs. In all
of them, Julia was graceful, shy, smiling yet somehow
elusive.

The next group were shots, some formal, some tabloid generated, of the courtship, engagement and marriage of the princess to Luigi di Vitale Ferrelli, from
whom, after an enormous scandal, she was now divorced. The young woman still smiled, still waved,
still appeared to be the gracious, kindly darling of the
tabloids, but as Laurie compared them with the early
photos, she kept getting the feeling that things were
not nearly as rosy for the princess.

Laurie frowned. Interesting. And Julia had been
virtually invisible since the divorce.

"Wouldn't it be weird to have grown up with this
kind of wealth?" Hawk said, flipping through a stack
of movies on disk. For the first time, Laurie noticed
there was a cheerful sort of flush on his cheekbones,
and he'd caught his long hair back away from his
face. A long wisp of hair drifted down to touch his
jaw. If she didn't know better, she'd say the man

was…happy. When he looked up, his vivid eyes glittered with green sparks. "Sorry, am I bothering you?"

She smiled. "Not at all. I'm obsessing in a way that's probably not productive."

He inclined his head slightly. "Are you nervous?"

"Yes." She lifted a shoulder. "Who wouldn't be?"

"You shouldn't be." He settled in the armchair just opposite her silk-clad knees and leaned forward earnestly, his elbows on his thighs. "People see what they expect to see—and you don't just look a little bit like the princess. You're practically twins." He grinned. "Really. You'll be fine."

Good grief. The grin transformed him entirely. His teeth, which she couldn't remember seeing before, were large and dazzlingly white and perfect. The grin made his eyes crinkle and turn upward at the corners, giving him a slightly wicked, elfish look. "You really ought to smile more often, Mr. Stone. I hardly recognize you."

"Well, I have to admit this is kind of fun. Like the movies or something." He looked at her. "I don't know what I was expecting—I mean, I know she's a royal and rich, but this—" he shook his head and looked around "—this is Robin Leach territory, you know? I'm not sure I really believed anyone lived like this."

"I know exactly what you mean," Laurie said. She touched the skirt of her suit. "You don't pay attention to women's shoes and clothing, but trust me, that's why these clothes are so fantastic, too. I couldn't buy this suit even if I went without eating for a year."

"Which would make the whole thing moot, anyway.'' The grin was more subdued this time, just one side of his mouth, but it was still excellent.

''I suppose it would.''

Francesco came into the room. ''The captain asked me to inform you that we will be landing in about forty minutes. Is there anything I can get for you?''

''No, thank you.''

When he nodded politely and retreated to the galley, Hawk put the CDs aside and said, ''So, you want to practice a little before we land?''

''Really? You don't mind?''

''Heck no.'' He winked. ''Tell all my buddies back home I hung out with a princess. They'll see my pictures in the tabloids and be jazzed.''

Laurie laughed. ''Thank you. I would like to practice.''

Chapter 7

Hawk was edgy as a Chicago limousine delivered them to the child care center. "Don't get out until I tell you to," he said to Laurie, and stepped out of the car, checking the scene with expert eyes. The crowd was huge, as he'd expected. The speaker area was carefully blocked off with sawhorses and police tape, with a wide, open area between the stage and the crowd. Standard procedure for a celebrity appearance. A comfortingly large cadre of police and FBI were visible, which meant there were more who were invisible.

The crowd itself was a mishmash—old and young, mostly middle class and lower; wealthy people were too sophisticated to stand outside on a hot June afternoon to catch a glimpse of a princess. A neat line of children, scrubbed and brushed and polished, in their very best clothes, waited onstage. Hawk smiled when he saw them. They were the ones who'd get a kick out of this. It made him the tiniest bit sad that it wasn't really the princess they'd be seeing—but he supposed they would never know.

He turned back. "All right, Princess Julia," he said, putting out a hand to help her. A graceful foot in a spectator pump, a fine, trim ankle, a long, long leg emerged—and the crowd sent up a cheer. "She's here! She's here!" Hawk saw them turning to each other, pointing and straining for a glimpse as Laurie emerged, trim and tall and impossibly well-groomed. She paused for a moment, removed the dark glasses, met his eyes for one long second, then smiled and waved.

Two agents came forward, flanking her on either side, and Hawk brought up the rear, scanning the crowd nearest the containment fence for signs of anything or anyone suspicious. But they were all just waving, some of them sticking their hands through the fence. Primed for this, Laurie reached out and touched some, stroked a baby's cheek, smiled and waved graciously.

They *loved* her.

Hawk had never understood the appeal of royalty. What was the big deal? Who cared, really, about such an archaic notion? But in the service, he'd spent a week in London with some of his buddies, not more than a year or two after Princess Diana had died, and he'd been amazed at the passion the common people felt for her. It was a phenomenon he associated with icons like the Virgin Mary, very popular in his part of the world—reverent and idealistic and somehow poignant. Walking behind Princess Julia, he felt an odd sort of fondness for the real woman. It had to be a strain, but she'd always been known for her kindness and generosity.

It made him feel even more protective. Protective of Laurie—as—Julia, but also of Julia herself, hidden away somewhere safe. He stepped a little closer as they climbed the steps to the makeshift stage.

The beautifully dressed children stood at a signal from their teacher as the entourage approached the stage, and Hawk was oddly moved by the dazzled expressions on their faces, particularly the girls. Laurie made a point of taking each little hand and smiling at them, one by one, increasing the level of illumination on one little girl's face to that of the sun.

The children sang a song, and then Laurie took the podium. Hawk suddenly didn't like the setup. It was too open, making her an easy mark for an assassin. The thought made his gut twist painfully, and he grimly scanned the crowd and the grounds for any suspicious movements, anyone pushing urgently through the assembly.

Standing at the podium, Laurie paused. The audience settled and waited breathlessly. Hawk did not look at her, afraid he'd transmit some of his nervousness. He worried that she might be very nervous herself now, and could not help listening as she began to speak.

It was flawless. She spoke in the dulcet, warm tones of the princess, her voice lilting perfectly in imitation of the Montebello accent. She made them cheer once and laugh once, and then it was over and they were clapping madly. She cut the ribbon for the center, the children sang another song, and then they were done, the princess, flanked by guards, making her way back to the limousine.

By the car waited a young girl, thirteen or fourteen years old. Her hair was smoothed into a bun and she wore a dress and a pair of modest high heels, but it was plain she was not well-to-do. There was a worn quality to everything she had on, and the shoes were imitation leather, scuffed at the toes.

"Princess Julia!" she cried, dashing around a security guard to present a piece of paper and a pen. "Can I have your autograph?"

Laurie shot an alarmed look at Hawk, and he understood immediately. She didn't know how to write in the princess's handwriting. He gave a single nod. *Do it anyway.*

She smiled, took the pen and wrote a short message—"Always believe in yourself. Princess Julia Sebastiani"—and then bent and kissed the girl on the cheek. The girl got misty eyed, and if Hawk were another kind of guy, he would have himself.

Safely inside the limo, Laurie fell against the back of the seat. "Oh, my God. That was one of the most terrifying things I've ever done."

He took her hand. "You were brilliant, Laurie. You even fooled me."

She raised her eyes. They were bluer than anything he'd ever seen. Bluer than the desert sky on a sunny day. Bluer than Easter eggs. "Really?" she asked quietly. And then added, "Those kids were something, weren't they?"

"Yeah," he said. "Yeah, they really were."

The two of them were taken to their hotel—and this time, there was a horde of photographers waiting when they arrived. Hawk saw Laurie take a deep breath as she put on her dark glasses. Lines of weariness showed around her mouth. "Protect me, kind sir.

I'm really getting tired now. All I want in the world is a nice, hot bath and my jeans.''

"Not long now.''

First they had to get through the crowd, mostly just curious people drawn by the limousine and the photographers to see who it might be. When she turned out not to be Brad Pitt or a rock star, most of them continued on their way quickly enough. Laurie and Hawk moved across the sidewalk into the hotel, where staff waited to whisk them quickly and without fanfare up to their suite. After making sure everything was all right, the employees departed, and Laurie kicked off her shoes and wandered over to the table, where an enormous fruit basket waited alongside a bottle of red wine. "Ooh, nice,'' she said, reading the label. "French merlot. This should be lovely. Are you a wine drinker?''

It was odd to see the princess and hear Laurie. "Not much of a drinker at all.''

She nodded, unbuttoning her jacket. Beneath it she wore a pale tank top, probably silk, judging by the sheen. Her arms were slim and straight, and when she moved back toward the windows, he found himself admiring her rear end and the line of her shoulders, her long legs. He was conscious of a certain restlessness, a wish to—

"Why don't you catch a bath and a nap?'' he suggested, picking up the channel changer. "I'm going to kick back and watch TV for a while. Need to charge our batteries while we can.''

Laurie took a bite of her apple, nodding a little distractedly. "In a few minutes. Did you see this view?''

"Didn't pay much attention.'' He turned on the

television, and it blared loudly for a second before he found the volume control on the remote.

"Come take a look. It's beautiful."

He didn't really want to go stand beside her and admire the view. Something about her was making him feel reckless, hungry, and resisting those feelings brought an edge of irritability. For one thing, was he responding to a fantasy—Laurie as the princess? Or was it something about Laurie herself?

She turned when he didn't move. "Really. Just a quick glimpse, and you can go back to the television."

He put the remote on the table and loosened his tie as he joined her at the window. Beneath them ran the Chicago River, with its span of bridges, and just beyond was Lake Michigan, very blue in the late afternoon sun. Boats and bright sails dotted the water, impossibly tiny from this distance. "It is nice," he admitted. "So much water in one place always kind of amazes me. From here you can see how vulnerable those tiny boats are, too, can't you?"

"Have you ever been out on a lake or the ocean like that?"

"Not really. Rode a ferry once across Puget Sound. That's about it." He noticed that her scent had changed. In place of the lemon-yellow freshness that ordinarily clung to her, she now smelled of something more exotic. Spicy. It made him think of the secret curves of a woman's body, the lower swell of a breast, the curve of a buttock, the back of her knee, and he took a breath. "You?"

"Lots. My father bought a boat when I was about fourteen, and we went camping at lakes and reservoirs all the time. I love water-skiing."

"That doesn't surprise me somehow."

She grinned, a purely American kind of sauciness in her face. "Yeah, I'm a healthy kind of girl, right?"

"Yeah," he said. "Well, uh, rounded."

"I choose," she said, "to take that as a compliment. For now." She reached up and let her hair down with a few deft gestures. It was full and curly from being pinned up all day, and it released a much-more-Laurie kind of smell—something clean, bright yellow, as sunny as she was. "I'm going to take a shower and that nap. See you afterwhile."

He went back to the couch. "All right."

He flipped through channels, hearing her move around in the bedroom, humming some cheerful child's ditty.

"Did they deliver our luggage?" Laurie said from behind him. "I can't find my personal bag."

"I don't know." He sat up, looking around, but there didn't appear to be any luggage anywhere. "I'll check my room. Maybe they put it all in one place."

And there it was, a little rolling overnight bag, square and black with lime-green piping. He carried it back to the room, but didn't see her immediately.

Then he did. She was bending over the minibar in the corner, and the straight skirt rode up on the back of her thighs. Bare thighs with supple skin and strong muscles—thighs he suddenly wanted to touch, leading to a rear end that was damned near perfect. Standing there in the middle of the room, Hawk had a very inappropriate vision of his hand pulling that skirt up to her waist and—

"Oh good!" she said, turning. "You found it." Noticing nothing amiss, she padded over to him in

her bare feet and bent forward to take the handle from
him. "I appreciate it."

He could see down her shirt. To a bra made of pale,
chocolate-colored lace that clasped a very pretty pair
of breasts. He jerked his gaze away. "Sure," he said
gruffly, moving away. He sat tensely on the couch
until he heard the water start in the bathroom, then
discreetly adjusted himself.

Laurie or the princess or the combination? He
hadn't been so easily aroused in about a hundred
years. Not a great situation, considering. But his
mind, to be difficult, flashed that picture of her skirt
once more, and he had to turn to the news to get it
out of his head.

It could be a long couple of weeks.

Laurie slept for nearly two hours. When she awakened, early evening sunlight streamed in the windows,
gauzy yellow against the sheers. The strain she'd been
holding in the muscles of her shoulders—never let it
be said that good posture was easy—had disappeared.
It was a relief to see her own face in the mirror when
she went in to brush her teeth, a relief to slip into a
pair of well-worn jeans and a simple, scoop-necked
T-shirt, and leave her hair down the way she was used
to it. It was also nice not to feel makeup clogging her
pores. She put some lip moisturizer on and went in
search of coffee to blow away the cobwebs in her
head, and something substantial to eat.

And Hawk. She tried to pretend she was looking
for him because he was her only companion. When
she came into the sitting area of the suite, she found
him asleep on the short couch, his stockinged feet
propped on the arm. His black hair spilled over an

embroidered pillow, silkier than anything the princess wore, and his face, ordinarily so guarded, was breathtakingly beautiful.

He was a very masculine man, but *beautiful* was the right word for his face. What else to name that perfect alignment of hard angles of brow and jaw and cheekbone, in relation to that generous mouth and elegantly drawn eyebrows and thick black lashes?

She discovered she had no wish to do anything but stand there and look at him, greedily devouring every detail. His long brown hand resting against his flat belly. His chin, so cleanly cut, above his throat. She wondered how it would smell if she nestled there.

He stirred a little, and she bolted toward the tiny coffeemaker on the counter. *Get it together, Laurie,* she told herself. *He's your partner. You don't want to start something that's only going to get your heart smashed.* Blindly, she opened the cellophane package of coffee-in-a-teabag the hotel provided.

That was the bottom line, wasn't it? Her roommate, Tanya, would be able to play with Hawk Stone for a couple of weeks and walk away from it unscathed. Tanya would take enormous pleasure in whatever she discovered, would laugh with him, please him in return, and then move on to the next adventure.

Laurie could not. She was smart enough to understand the fact that casual sex had always seemed like an oxymoron to her. Impossible to open yourself up so much to another person and expect that it wouldn't leave a mark. Therefore, a person had to be careful about who she got that close to, and where and why.

The trouble was there were definitely sparks between them. They'd nearly exploded last night in his room, and this morning would have led to something more if she hadn't rebuffed him. She hadn't missed the look on his face when they got to the hotel this afternoon. He wanted her, but he wasn't much happier about it than she was.

The timing of his attraction suddenly struck her. Maybe he wanted the princess? The thought made her smile. How weird was that? Even weirder than the schism she was feeling, balanced between being herself and being the princess.

Measuring water into the baby-size coffeepot, she mulled over the possibility that he was attracted to the princess, not necessarily to her. Would it be possible to treat Hawk as part of the job—indulge her wish to explore the intensity of such a man without getting hurt, by doing it as the princess instead of herself?

Which presented some interesting ethical questions. Was it right to do it as the princess if the princess wouldn't?

But Laurie would never know, would she?

And what if Hawk fell in love with the princess? Then he'd be the one hurt at the end of it.

Very confusing. And therefore not a great idea.

"Hey," said the voice of a rake, softly raspy from sleep, and even more impossibly deep and musical. "That coffee sucks, you know. Let's just order some from room service."

Startled, she nearly dropped the pot. "You have to quit scaring me like that," she said, recovering.

"I didn't mean to. Sorry." He sat up and reached for his boots. "When did I do it before?"

Laurie realized he didn't know she'd dropped her blush in the sink this morning when he knocked at her bedroom door. Maybe she should just stay away from sinks for the duration. "I don't know," she said, and put the pot on the counter. "Let's do order from room service. Dinner, too. You have to be as hungry as I am by now."

He was already pulling the menu toward him. "What's your pleasure, madam?"

The phone rang. Hawk answered it with a gruff hello, wiggling his eyebrows to show he'd done it on purpose. He listened for a minute and said, "The princess was just saying it was time for dinner. Yes." He listened. "That sounds great. Bring a giant pot of coffee, too, with cream." He looked at Laurie, who mouthed, *milk,* and he added, "Some low-fat milk, too, please. And turbinado sugar."

He hung up. "Well, it appears their chef is most eager to show off his skills, and has prepared a meal for us. It will be here shortly, so you might want to scramble into something princessy for a few minutes."

Laurie wrinkled her nose. "Surely even a princess lets her hair down once in a while."

"I'm sure she does." He grinned. "But I bet she lounges in something besides jeans and bare feet. Didn't Mrs. Watson buy you some mules or something?"

"Yeah. Let me go see what I can do. But let's get rid of them as fast as we can so I can go back to being me, okay?"

He held up a hand. "Promise."

Laurie scuttled off to decide what Julia would wear when she was relaxing. As she opened the closet to find her things all neatly hung and pressed—a level of service she would never have imagined—she felt a creeping sense of temptation come over her. It was a good chance to test her theory that Hawk was attracted to the princess. She'd be the princess through dinner, then change back to herself afterward, to see if the idea held water.

Not smart, said a little voice from the back of her mind. Laurie dismissed it, trying to decide what to put on. There was little casual wear here, because of course they hadn't needed it, but there was a nice pair of leather mules that wouldn't look weird with jeans, and a long-sleeved blouse, quietly tailored, of the lightest possible linen. It had about ten thousand tiny buttons up the front, and she left a few more undone than she probably should have. With her stark-white bra beneath, it was understatedly sexy. With the high-heeled leather sandals, her legs looked a million miles long, and she swept her hair up casually in a clasp. A little berry lipstick and she stepped back, transformed.

Wow. She was starting to like this. It was fun to be someone else for a while.

Hawk had relaxed a little when Laurie woke up after her nap. In her simple T-shirt and jeans she looked a lot more like someone's little sister than a princess, and therefore not quite so overwhelming.

And he discovered he missed the sexual lure of lusting after her in that little gold skirt. When he sent her back to her room for a change of clothes, he'd been wickedly hoping to continue his low-level arousal through the evening. It was something to do. And as long as he didn't make any overt moves, he suspected Laurie would never even notice.

A knock at the door announced their food had arrived, and automatically, Hawk unholstered his gun as he looked through the peephole. A cadre of servers stood there in white coats, and he opened the door with a scowl. "Not all of you can come in here. Pick two."

There were seven of them, and the oldest protested, speaking with an accent Hawk couldn't quite identify. "But, sir, we must all be present or we cannot properly serve such an elaborate repast!"

"No way," he said. "Sorry. Security risk is just too high. Which two are going to stay?"

Two youths, both black, one lean and rangy, the other round as a turtle, stepped back. "We're good."

"No," said the older man. "George," he said to the chubby youth, "you serve with me." He inclined his head. "The rest of you may return to your duties."

George rolled the large cart into the room and shook out a tablecloth over the table by the windows. Evening was thickening now, the light over the lake turning a brilliant gold in preparation for sunset. The snowy-white cloth seemed to take bits of the gold light into itself, an effect trebled by the crystal vase of sunflowers and yellow roses the youth settled to one side. Efficiently, he laid out china and silver and cloth napkins, heavy crystal tumblers, wineglasses and bread plates, then stepped back to wait for his boss to give him the next directive.

Except at that moment Laurie came out of the room, smiling that hovering, shivery smile as Julia. She stepped right into a long beam of the golden light, and it seemed to kiss her crown and dance downward, illuminating the curves of her lips and breasts and hips, skating over a cheekbone and the almost invisible gold chain that somehow drew attention to the valley of her breasts without appearing to be the slightest bit overt.

The youth's mouth opened. Then shut. Then he looked at his boss and back at the princess and simply stood there, as starstruck as anyone Hawk had ever seen.

"Hello," she said warmly, holding out her hand. "I understand you mean to serve us something wonderful. I am looking forward to it tremendously."

The youth took her hand and shook it like an automaton. The main chef, not to be outdone, bowed with a courtliness that made Hawk think of men in buckled shoes. "Your highness, it is our great honor to bring you a feast even the old gods would envy. Will you sit and let us serve you?"

"Thank you." She settled and allowed the older man to put the napkin in her lap. "Hawk?"

"Oh." He was nearly as starstruck as the boy. "Right. Sorry."

It wasn't really his kind of food, though he had to admit it was pretty. An appetizer of little veggies in a lemon sauce was followed by a crustless spinach tart and roasted chicken breasts with some sort of elusive sauce. The servers set each course down, filled wineglasses, then stepped away.

Hawk found it uncomfortable to have them standing there, just this side of hovering. Laurie, however, was quite pleasant to them when they served, and complimented the taste and presentation of the dishes, but otherwise ignored them and made light conversation with Hawk in the princess's voice. The whole thing gave him a strange disorientation. He knew that Laurie, the real person beneath the act, had to be as intimidated as he was, albeit laughing inwardly. But the elegant Princess facade never slipped for a single instant.

"I do love tarts," she said, her head gracefully floating on that long neck as she savored a tiny bite of one. "This is not your usual fare, though, is it?"

Hawk grinned. "No." He met her eyes and thought he saw a sparkle of amusement in the vivid blue irises, the hint of a nostril quivering. "Give me a good hamburger anyday." He was hungry enough, however, that he ate every bite. "I have to admit it's pretty good, though. Just not enough of it."

"Oh, have another serving, then, by all means!" Now he was sure he saw the wicked laughter lurking in her eyes. She turned. "Gentlemen, please bring my friend another serving of chicken and tart. He is a man and needs a little more than I."

Hawk lifted one eyebrow, promising revenge. He was hungry enough that he didn't turn it away, but he nearly choked when she said without guile, "Do tell me, Mr. Stone—are there native dishes among your people?"

He turned his face toward the windows to hide threatening laughter, and kicked Laurie beneath the table. Focusing with all his might on a single white sailboat making its way back to dock, he managed to pull himself together, take a deep breath and say, "Sure. Ever eaten fry bread?"

"No! Is it wonderful?" Now she looked a little more curious.

"Yeah," he said honestly. "Not fancy, you know—just big flat pieces of fried dough, but it's great stuff. We put honey on it, but people eat it all kinds of ways, with beans and cheese or with stew.

We ate mutton stew when I was little, before we moved to town.''

"And stews are very similar across the world, are they not? Meat to give flavor, whatever vegetables happen to be easy to keep, spices and water?''

A little silence fell, and Laurie shot him a look. It was his turn to keep the conversation going.

But just then, the chefs came forward. "Now for the final glory,'' said the old one. "A lemon ricotta cake. Low-fat and quite delicious. We think you will agree.''

"Thank you,'' Laurie said. "I am quite weary just now. We'll serve ourselves the cake and coffee.''

"Of course, of course.'' They cleared away the remains of the meal, set the cake on the table between Hawk, and nestled the wine in its bucket of ice. "Will there be anything else?''

"No, thank you. I will be sure to commend your talents to my father and the hotel management. The meal was excellent.''

Visible pleasure crossed the older man's face. The youth behind him looked anxiously at the princess, biting his lip. Hawk caught Laurie's eye and shifted his gaze to the young man. She smiled. "Is there something I might do for you, George?''

He shot a worried glance toward the boss, who scowled. "We do not need anything,'' George said majestically. "It was an honor merely to serve you, your highness.''

"A little memento, perhaps?'' Laurie persisted. "Mr. Stone. Is the Polaroid available?''

"Sure.'' It was something the FBI had wanted—a shot of each of the events where she spoke, as a method of record keeping. Hawk fetched the camera from his bedroom. The youth was trying hard to keep his excitement under control, but failed miserably. His face glowed as Laurie stood beside him and smiled. An incandescent grin broke out on his face, and his back was very straight as Hawk clicked the shutter. "Thank you," George said.

To the older man, Hawk said, "You, too, Chef."

He looked sour and alarmed. "Oh, no. I couldn't—"

Laurie gave him that princess smile and held out her hand. "It would give me great pleasure," she said. "Please."

Harrumphing, he allowed himself to be talked into it, standing with dignity next to Laurie, his pate shining with reflected light from the setting sun.

Hawk looked through the lens and felt as if he was kicked in the chest. Light haloed Laurie's very dark hair, suddenly edged her neck, and she winked at him discreetly, smiling her own smile as he clicked the picture—a more robust and mischievous expression than had ever been captured on the face of the reserved princess.

Again the schism caught him, but this time in a pleasant way. She was good, this neophyte agent. Somewhere during the past couple of days he'd learned to respect her. She was faced with a tough job and she was doing it well. If she also looked fabulous in the clothes of a princess, who could blame a man for noticing?

The two men finally took their leave, and the first thing Laurie did was pull the pins out of her hair. "Ouch," she said, rubbing her scalp. "Hairpins are annoying."

She settled back at the table. "Come on, big boy.

Let's pig out." Cutting into the cake, she served them both enormous slices and poured fresh coffee. "Oh, and turn on the news. I bet we made it on the local channel."

Hawk found the remote, turned the screen to face them, and sat back down with her. Outside, the light was fading over the lake, and she snapped on a lamp. Her hair fell in soft waves around her face, and he noticed immediately the difference in her posture. This was Laurie again, leaning back in her chair, her long, long legs crossed at the knee. One foot swung a backless, high-heeled sandal loosely. She ate the cake with great enjoyment, watching the screen for signs of their appearance.

And quite against his will, he noticed that the lamp cast an entirely different sort of light on her than the sunset had. It shone through the thin linen of her blouse to reveal every curve of her torso. With an alarming vividness, his imagination gave him a picture of his fingers sliding along that curve, lifting the flesh.

She seemed to feel his scrutiny all of a sudden. "What?"

He shook his head. "Nothing."

The television made a warning sound, and a red banner rolled across the bottom of the screen. "Ugh," Laurie said. "Tornado warning." She scowled and looked out the window to the sky. "Not close to here, I don't think. Where is London, Illinois?"

"No idea."

"I hate tornadoes," she said. "Ever been in one?"

"No. They don't really show up in the Southwest. Not enough humidity, I guess." He tasted the cake. "God, this is excellent!"

"It is."

"Have you ever been in a tornado?" he asked.

"In Nebraska? Yeah." A shadow, surprising on the sunny features, crossed her face. "A bad one when I was twelve. That's how I fell out of the loft of the barn." She pointed in the vague direction of her scarred arm. "Tornado sucked me right out of the window."

"Holy—er—cow. Really?"

"Yep. I was hiding from my brothers with my Barbie dolls. That was the one place they never looked me, you know? My parents had heard the warnings and tried to find me, but that twister came up fast and they had to take cover before they had a chance to search the barn." Her eyes grew distant, and Hawk wondered what she was seeing in memory. "It was like some giant hand grabbed me and threw me down on the ground. I was lucky, really. The break was bad, but it could have been a lot worse."

"Whew. I guess." He helped himself to more cake. "I've never seen a tornado," he said. "It must be impressive."

"That's one word for it," she said dryly. "Count your blessings."

But now he was curious. "What does it look like?"

"Before or after?"

"During."

"It's hard to explain. Mainly it's a lot of damned noise. They're unbelievably loud, and dirty. You've never seen such a mess." She put her fork down. "That was so good.... There must be some storms in the desert," she continued. "Not everyone has tornadoes, but there are hurricanes on the coast, other kinds of violent storms. What do you get in the desert?''

''Thunderstorms, I guess, and the flash floods that come with them. But if you have the brains of a gnat, you stay out of arroyos and away from low-lying roads after a big storm. People don't always.''

''Of course.''

He'd made enough of a pig of himself, he decided, and leaned back. The red warning beeped again across the bottom of the screen, more urgent now. ''I guess the difference between tornadoes and all the other violent kinds of weather is that you can prepare for the rest of them. Even earthquakes, to a degree—better buildings and that kind of thing. But a tornado—how can you prepare for anything that can hit like an atomic blast?''

She looked slightly green all of a sudden. ''You know what? I don't think I want to talk about this anymore.''

He grinned. ''Okay. No problem.''

''What I'd like to know, if you don't mind, Hawk, is what happened to your partner? Is that too personal?''

Maybe it was the good food, the good company, the fact that he was nearly two thousand miles from the scene of the crime. Maybe it was just his wish to make up for putting that slightly sick look on her face. ''No,'' he said, and took a breath. Maybe it would be good to say it out loud, see what it felt like now.

Still, he felt tension in his neck as he let the memory out of the back of his brain, calling it up deliberately for the first time, not counting when he'd had to tell the police psychologist. ''It was a domestic violence call,'' he said. ''Came in about three in the afternoon. A winter Tuesday. It was snowing a little as we got there, really pretty snow. Big flakes. The house seemed quiet, but that doesn't always mean anything, you know.'' He looked at his hands, spread his fingers apart, aware on some level that he missed police work.

''A neighbor had called it in, and there had been a record of other calls to that address, so we were particularly careful. You always are on DV calls—you wouldn't believe how many cops are injured and killed in domestic violence situations every year.'' He shook his head. His eye twitched faintly and he put a finger to it.

''Hawk, if it's too disturbing, you don't have to talk about it.''

He raised his eyes, seeing the compassion on her face. She reached over the table and put her hand on his. ''I'm sorry to have opened that wound.''

He looked away, drew his hand out from under hers, not unkindly. Now that he'd begun, he felt compelled to say the rest. ''We were on the sidewalk when we heard screaming and crashes from inside, and we both ran toward the house—it was the kind of screaming that lets you know it's really, really bad.'' He paused. ''You just don't forget that kind of scream.

''John went first, drawing his gun, and it all just went so fast from that second that I can never quite get it straight exactly how it happened, you know? I saw the kid first—he was a little kid, trying to get the gun from his dad, and I dived for him, without thinking about anything else. The perp fired. The mother was the one screaming. She was backed into a corner and had tears running down her face, and the guy was drunk, and he fired. I saw the round hit John, and I held on to the kid, keeping his head against my chest so he wouldn't do anything stupid, you know? And by the time I got a clear shot at the dad, he'd killed his wife and turned the gun on himself.''

Hawk fell silent, staring at his hands. Aside from the psychologist and the official reports, he hadn't said the whole thing aloud like that before. ''It was over in thirty seconds. Three dead bodies and this four-year-old boy who'd just lost both of his parents in a way that was gonna scar him for life, and there was my partner, dead the second he hit the floor.''

A roiling wave of emotion came over Hawk and he bent forward to put his head in his hands, afraid he'd be sick. ''I've been a cop for a few years now, and seen my share of murders and bad accident scenes, but you just can't imagine how bad that was. All I could do for the longest time was hold that kid, who was crying so hard he couldn't catch his breath. I finally picked him up and carried him outside. I threw up and so did he, and we called it in.''

''Hawk, that's the saddest story I've ever heard. I'm so sorry.''

He looked up and saw there were tears streaming down Laurie's face. Tears of pity. Her eyes were nearly neon under the salty wash, and when he looked up, she reached across the table toward his hand. A sense of himself dissolving, turning to sand to be blown away in the wind, returned. He could almost see the molecules of himself spinning away—distancing him from the brutal reality of a world where a father could commit murder in front of his son. From everything and everyone who was a part of such a world.

He heard a roar in his ears. Gunshots and crying and disbelief. A low, cold tremor shook his body.

How could it still be so bad?

He jerked away when her hand touched his arm. He knew how he must look—sniveling and lost, a man with no spine, breaking under the pressure of plain, brutal reality. It just was. His father hadn't collapsed, had he? Hell, he'd made it through Vietnam. He'd probably seen a million things worse than that day in January.

"Let me get you a shot of whiskey," Laurie said. "What d'you say?" She was already rising, moving away from the table, and he was triply humiliated to want her, to ache over those long legs in heels and jeans, to want to rip that airy little blouse right off her body. He'd take her right there on the Persian carpet, with a thousand dollars in gold around her neck and nothing else.

The vision made him sick. What kind of world held such disparity? That one child should be tended so exquisitely and another so badly?

"I don't need a nurse," he said. "Thought I was talking to a partner, not a nursemaid."

She whirled. "That wasn't fair."

"Yeah, well, that's life, huh?" He clicked off the television and stalked toward his room. "I'll leave you alone."

She crossed her arms. "*Excellent* idea."

Chapter 8

It took some doing, but Laurie managed to talk herself into a good space by morning. She had a job to do. It was an excellent opportunity for her to advance her career, and she was confident she was doing an outstanding job so far. No man could be allowed to get in her way.

They were slated to be in Dallas for a multinational gala this evening, and according to an intelligence update, there was a lot of hope among the superiors who had arranged the operation that the kidnappers might reveal themselves. Before she emerged from her bedroom that morning, Laurie carefully considered what she would wear for the evening, and packed it on top so that it could be whisked out for a quick pressing when they arrived at the Dallas hotel. She made sure which accessories she would need, as well. She chose a dress in shades of graduated green, with a fitted bodice and full skirt, and an airy wrap for her shoulders. Her gun could slip into a holster on her thigh, and none would be the wiser.

For the trip, she chose a suit much like the one she'd worn yesterday, this one shell-pink. Laurie wondered if the princess ever got tired of these anemic color choices. The suit was great, but Laurie would have liked it in a vivid red or maybe yellow. Especially with her hair this dark. Which she had to admit she liked. Who knew it could make so much difference to change your hair color a few shades? Reluctantly, she arranged that hair in a French braid and laced it with a set of shell pins.

And she used her own cologne. The princess's didn't suit her. Funny that she could adopt every other thing in a woman's repertoire but this. But it likely didn't matter much. It was entirely possible the princess had come up with some new scent during her two years of seclusion. She might have picked up a lot of new things, come to that.

Oddly, that one little realization gave Laurie a lot more confidence all of a sudden. She'd always known it intellectually, but now it gave her a sense of relief and freedom. As long as she didn't do anything rash, the little things would be dismissed as the new mannerisms of a woman the public had not seen in two years.

Hawk was not in the sitting room when she emerged, dressed and ready to go. A silver coffeepot on a tray with a single red rose sat on the table, along with a basket of assorted pastries, cheeses and fruits. Gratefully, she settled and poured herself a cup, delicately sliced a pear and chose several kinds of cubed cheese.

In the other room, she heard the shower, and she

tried hard not to imagine how that long body looked under the stream. But even if she was modestly successful in avoiding an actual picture, she still felt an odd stirring down her spine.

Hawk Stone. She sighed, looking out the window to the lake. What a puzzle he was! Prickly and kind by turns, irritating and deliciously sexy. Such a *man* in some ways, too. A woman who had experienced such a traumatic event would talk and cry through it, letting the bubbles of sorrow and horror out a little at a time until there was nothing left to ferment, as was happening within Hawk.

She watched a boat chugging out from shore, leaving triangles of wake behind it. Last night, she'd changed her assessment somewhat. Hawk wasn't by nature a brooder. He didn't, as a rule, take himself too seriously. He was simply a man who had not recovered from a blow. And although he'd hurt her feelings last night by pushing her away, she wondered now if there might be some way she could help him through this stage, so that when the two weeks were over he could return to something like a normal life. Or at least begin to.

In a way, she supposed it was arrogant to think that she had the tools, but she did. It was her very optimism that would help her.

Just then, he emerged from his room on a cloud of man-smelling dampness, his hair wet and slicked back from his gorgeous face, his feet bare. He wore a pair of black slacks and a crisp white shirt with a tie crisscrossed with red and blue lines, and Laurie realized once again that she *wanted* him, in a way that was purely alien to her. Wanted him with a base kind of physicality that slightly embarrassed her.

"Morning," he said in that beautiful voice as he poured coffee into a cup. "Sleep well?"

"Fine, thank you. And you?" She stirred sugar into her own cup.

He took a pair of socks from where they'd been hanging on his belt and put one on. "Not that great."

"I'm sorry to hear that." His feet were as beautiful as his hands. Long, elegant toes; smooth brown skin over high arches...

"My own fault." He put the other sock on, tugged on his boots and turned to face her. His eyes were so green it nearly hurt to look at them, and they were fixed like a searchlight on Laurie's face, the expression in them more open than any she'd seen thus far.

Her heart lurched. Oh, he was so dangerous! Just sitting here like this with him made her feel alert and reckless, made her nerves respond in the most irritating way. It would be, she decided, a very bad idea to reach out to him, even if she thought she could help him. It was just too dangerous for her. Too much of a threat of real pain at the end of this. She said nothing.

"Laurie, I was a jerk last night, and I'm sorry."

She lifted a shoulder. "You'll forgive me, but I'm really not interested in a cycle of fighting and making up. So I suggest we forget trying to be friends and just agree that we see the world in different terms. At most, this assignment will last two weeks, half of which is already gone."

His jaw tightened. "If that's what you want."

"It is. We'll keep this as professional as possible and thereby avoid any problems."

"Thereby?" His mouth quirked up on one side.

Laurie softened a little. "Sounds lawyerly, don't you think?"

"I get it." He filled a plate with a variety of pastries and poured orange juice from a carafe. "Let's review the coming day, then. I had a talk this morning with some of the security detail that's been assigned to assist us, and there are a couple of things you need to know."

"All right."

As he launched into the details, Laurie told herself this was for the best. Professional relationship only. But as he told her about the gathering this evening, brought her attention to dossiers they would have to go over on the flight, she found herself watching his mouth as it moved, looking at his hands, wishing—

Just wishing.

Thick clouds made the landing in Dallas very bumpy, but other than that, the trip was uneventful. Laurie reviewed the names and faces of the principals who would be in attendance at the gala—and had Hawk read out the list to test her on her knowledge. He then took the photos of people the princess would recognize and tested her on those. She got all but one—an Egyptian named Farouk Bashir. She kept reversing it.

At the hotel, they separated easily and dressed in their respective rooms. Since they would be leaving again first thing in the morning, not much unpacking needed to be done. Laurie showered and arranged her hair, called in a manicurist to fix a nail she'd broken, and had a small snack. She dressed with the care she'd learned to take, but then felt nervous at the amount of chest the neckline of the gown showed. It seemed like a *lot*.

One of Mrs. Watson's concerns had been that the princess was bustier than Laurie, and a good deal of thought had gone into the undergarments to wear with necklines such as this. Laurie had protested that she didn't need all that—who would pay attention? And Mrs. Watson had insisted that men always remembered a good bust, and in these circles, a décolletage was more or less required. A thin waist and good décolletage.

So Laurie had acquiesced. And she'd had a taste of what it might be like when she'd tried on the red gown. But alone in her room tonight, looking at herself in the mirror, she felt like a complete imposter. The bra made a lot of her bust, set off by a delicate emerald at her neck. She had genuine cleavage. It was the only thing she saw when she looked in the mirror—the white rise of breasts above the gown. It made her think of period films. Thank goodness for the wrap, she thought, draping it over her shoulders.

She was a little shy emerging from the bedroom, but for a moment her worries were forgotten, because Hawk himself had been transformed into an elegant, unbelievably handsome man. His hair was slicked back from his face into a ponytail at his neck, and he wore a black tuxedo. The white shirt made his face look darker, and his eyes glowed like marbles. Laurie whistled, raising her eyebrows. "Wow, you look fabulous."

He lifted his chin, completely at ease. "Thanks." He looked her over. "So do you. But I gotta ask, where's the gun?"

Wickedly, Laurie bent and lifted the hem of her

skirt, pulling it up to reveal the holster strapped to her stockinged thigh. "Special issue." She grinned. "Pretty hot, huh?"

"You can let the hem down now."

She grinned even more. "What's the matter, Hawk? Too much for you?"

"Nothing is too much for me, honey," he said. His eyes went smoky as his gaze stroked the length of her leg. "But we're supposed to be professionals here, and maybe that's not all that professional."

Flushing a little, she dropped her skirt. "True." She brushed at her face, but her hair was pinned away, glittering with little emeralds she'd scattered through it. "On a purely professional level, Mr. Stone, I'm a bit nervous and would like your opinion on this dress. Too much?"

"No." He bit the word off, and pulled up his sleeve to look at his watch. "We do need to get going. You'll be fine."

"Okay." Showtime again. "This could get fairly exhausting, you know."

"Maybe we'll get lucky and it'll all be over tonight."

She nodded. "Yeah, maybe."

Hawk disliked the setup of the gala immediately. The thousand-dollar-a-plate fund-raiser had been arranged by a local senator who was said to have aspirations to the presidency. But the security, while in evidence, was not nearly strict enough in Hawk's opinion. The situation made him edgy from the moment of their arrival.

First of all, the event was being held in a famous old restaurant set amid an acre of trees. Shrubs lined the walls of the transformed mansion, and an endless number of doors opened to little porches and patios around the whole thing. Lights glittered in the trees and illuminated each doorway, but the plethora of openings made him uneasy.

The building was crowded with dignitaries and their spouses, their voices raised in that bright, high-toned roar cut through with the clink of glassware. It was a perfumed and glittering assembly, elegant and civilized, making burly, unsmiling bodyguards all the more evident.

Laurie, flanked immediately by members of the FBI team sent out as extra security, growled at him. "You've got to make them back off a little bit. I'm here to circulate."

She was right, but Hawk didn't have to like it. He had a word with the head of the team anyway, promising to stick by Laurie every second himself, as would be expected of a royal bodyguard. For an hour, he followed her grimly from room to room, listening as she made small talk with those who came forward to greet her. One after another wanted to touch the young, beautiful princess's hand; offer condolences over her brother, presumed dead, renew their acquaintance with her after her long hiatus from the public eye.

At last the guests were led into a room as wide as the house, with French doors open all the way along the back on both sides. Security guards were posted at each one, but Hawk saw no evidence of anyone being checked—guests trailed in and out at will. His anxiety increased. With tension tightening his neck, he scanned the people around them, seeing only the powdered and shaved and largely white faces of the well-to-do gathering.

A cluster of young men stared openly at the princess, clearly wishing they could get a little closer, have a chance to charm her. One finally broke through the knot around Laurie. He was a smooth one, as polished as any prep school dandy. "Your highness," he said in a deep baritone. "My name is Jacob Peltier. We met many years ago at Cannes, though of course you wouldn't remember."

Laurie allowed him to take her hand, smiling up at him with a perfect imitation of Julia's sweetness. "Of course I do. How are you?"

Peltier tucked Laurie's hand into the crook of his elbow, and Hawk felt a flash of blinding jealousy when the man bent a little too close, subtly looking down her dress. Hawk had to restrain himself from shoving the ape away; even the thought of the man's breath on her offended him. Grimly, he set his jaw and went back to examining the crowd for anything even slightly amiss. The thick crowd made it difficult to see, but the guests were beginning to disperse throughout the room, taking their places at the tables, set with heavy white linen and crystal.

The program was simple and informal—a number of dignitaries and notables seated at tables throughout the room would be called upon, one at a time, to deliver a few words at the start of dinner. The luckiest guests gained a seat at one of the more popular tables, and the audience of an ambassador or celebrity.

Or a princess.

Hawk found himself growing more and more alert, his nerves prickling furiously as more people milled into the big room. The suave young man, plainly a child of enormous wealth, laughed at something Laurie said and silkily tucked her closer to his side. Hawk simmered and tried to ignore it, telling himself the man was extra protection just now. Anyone who wanted to kidnap her would have to fight him to get her.

The acoustics exaggerated the sounds of the party guests, and he didn't like the way people kept crowding up to Laurie, two and three and four deep. They were civilized enough, but Hawk found it hard to keep track of who was touching her, what threats might be presented by the thick crowds all around them as the human traffic streamed into the banquet room. The back of his neck grew hot with sweat, and he found his gaze darting from one dark-eyed man to a woman in a sari, checking expressions, hand movements, odd exchanges in the crowd.

Hawk moved so that he was right behind her, his hand on the small of her back, his other loose and ready in case he had to pull a weapon. And even with all that diligence, he didn't see the trouble start until it was too late.

Laurie felt Hawk against her back, felt the tenseness in his body, and had to admit the scene was giving her the same hyperalert sense of danger. The crowd was a nightmare of security, and anyone who knew Dallas would know what a perfect opportunity it would be for an assault on the princess. They were too close to the doors that led to the dense growth just beyond. There were too many people, too few security personnel.

She found herself balancing a double role—agent and princess. Her legs and arms felt springy and ready for anything, while at the same time she had to remember to glide, to hold her head just so, to keep that trademark smile dancing over her mouth. And to flirt with the rather slimy young man who kept pressing his arm into her breast as if she wouldn't recognize what he was doing. He was too close, his breath, smelling of fennel, brushing over her chin and mouth.

She couldn't imagine Julia finding anything remotely appealing about him, but one never knew the tastes of another woman's heart. Perhaps they'd once been lovers or shared chaste kisses in some hidden cove. "Will you be in Dallas long?" he asked, sliding her arm more closely against him. He tried not to be obvious about it, but she saw him looking down the front of her dress, and she resisted bringing up a hand to cover herself, though she did adjust the wrap a tiny bit.

In fits and starts they filtered in, and Laurie kept up her end of the flirtation in a ladylike manner, smiling gently. "Oh, no. We leave tonight."

"Oh, yes, the publicity tour. It must be exhausting. Perhaps we could meet in Aspen when you finish? Have dinner."

"Perhaps," she said.

A matron moved up on the other side of Jacob, offering a greeting. Laurie answered with a smile, wondering if she ought to know this person or not. By now they'd all blurred together—one polished, slim, silver-haired woman blending with the next, one tuxedoed dignitary's accent indistinguishable from another.

It was claustrophobic and tense. A muscle in her shoulder was so tight it hurt. Then, with a few more steps, they were out of the worst of the crush, heading for their assigned seats. Laurie saw a large, engraved card in a silver holder proclaiming her spot, and with a quick smile, headed determinedly for it. She wasn't quite able to shake Jacob Peltier, and resigned herself to sitting next to him through the dinner. She would just have to take a long hot shower when she was finished here, and wash off the slightly soiled feeling he was giving her.

A sudden stir in the crowd behind her made Hawk let go, and Laurie turned, nerves crackling, to see what the fuss was. There was a shout, a sudden backward jostling of bodies, and Jacob clasped her arm tightly. For once she did not object, and leaned into the safety of his body as they passed a set of French doors.

But suddenly he was no longer simply holding her arm, but was steering her toward the entrance, his other hand over her mouth. "Not a word," he said, and ducked into the night, clasping her waist so hard she couldn't get any leverage.

Laurie didn't lose her head. The entire purpose was for the princess to be kidnapped, after all. She allowed herself to be half dragged into the dense shrubbery lining the walls, into the shadows of the trees beyond. The air smelled thickly of roses.

And then the hand that was holding her was suddenly tearing at the front of her dress, groping and mauling her as he bent down and bit her neck. Laurie reacted instantaneously. With a furious cry, she whipped around and clocked him with a left to the jaw, using all her considerable strength. She felt her fist connect, and when he reeled back in pain, she stomped on his foot and jabbed her elbow into his diaphragm.

"Help!" she cried. "Help me!" And she dashed out of the thicket, only then becoming aware of how much of her skin was visible. She scrambled to cover herself, thinking wildly that he'd ripped her bodice and she was exposed.

Then it was over. Jacob was hauled out of the thicket by a pair of security guards, and Hawk was beside her, draping her with his coat. His gun was drawn and he growled orders with enough ferocity that the crowd parted instantly in front of them. Like Moses and the Red Sea, she thought.

"Damn," she said when they reached the sidewalk outside. "That was so out of character for the princess. I should never have hit him. She wouldn't have done it that way. Not with a fist. I bet her brother was not as obnoxious as mine."

"Laurie, we don't have to talk about it right now, okay?"

"Fine, but it was—"

"Nothing," he said, and hustled her into the limo.

Laurie settled, scowling, next to the window, staring out at the sudden surge of action with dismay. She'd handled that very, very badly. What *would* the princess have done in such a situation? It was hard to imagine. Laurie didn't think she was the sort of woman who would put up with that kind of treatment, but it wasn't exactly like a princess to clock a man with a left to the jaw.

Hawk wordlessly handed her a handkerchief, and she realized that she tasted blood. Testing the place on her lip, she scowled again. Great. The black eye was nearly gone and now she'd look like she'd been brawling again.

Some princess. She frowned and pressed the handkerchief to her mouth, surprised when it hurt. From her purse, she took a compact and used the mirror to examine the spot. ''I didn't even feel that.'' She lifted the mirror to look at her neck. ''He *bit* me.'' The place throbbed a little, and it was oddly disgusting.

''I didn't pick up anything from him. Not a damned thing.'' Hawk peered out the window grimly. ''I'm sorry.''

''It's not your fault, Hawk.'' She put her hand on his leg. ''I didn't see it coming, either. He was good.''

Hawk looked at her and reached over to tug the coat together. ''The dress is destroyed.''

Laurie looked down. ''Turn your head.'' She opened the coat to see the tatters of thin fabric, shredded to reveal the bra beneath. Nothing else showed, just her breasts, sitting up high in chocolate lace. A thumbprint marked her, and with a strange little ripple of revulsion, her mind flashed back to the way she'd been mauled, her attacker's hand on her breasts, such a private place. She swore. ''That was gross,'' she said, and tucked the loose fabric into the edges of her bra as best she could.

Her hands were shaking. She took a deep breath and blew it out, mashing the handkerchief into a little ball in her fist, staring determinedly out the window until her emotional reaction settled. She'd be damned if she'd let Hawk see that it had upset her.

''Here,'' he said, handing her a glass with a measure of amber liquid in the bottom. ''Drink up. It'll help.''

She looked at it for a minute and wanted to take it, but was afraid he would see how she was trembling, a reaction that was moving from her hands up into her shoulders. ''In a minute.''

He swore vividly. "You see what I mean now? This isn't a game. It's dangerous."

"Would you mind not yelling at me just this minute?"

But his anger braced her, and she grabbed the glass from his hand, downed it in a single gulp and gave him back the glass. It burned, but it helped, too. "One more, I think."

He poured a measure, then one for himself. "You did a good job, Laurie," he said gruffly. "I'm pissed that the security was so bad."

"That's the idea, though, right? That we lured out the kidnappers?"

"I guess we'll find out, won't we?" He drank his shot, put the glass down firmly. "Did he hurt you?"

"No. I'm all right."

His jaw went hard. "Do you mind if I take a look?"

"A look?" She blinked. Lifted her face to him.

He was very close, and the recognition of that fact gave Laurie an unwelcome little jolt. He put his hand gently under her chin, examining her face, then her lips, minutely, his gaze intent and troubled, his mouth hard. He lifted her hair to look at the place where Jacob had bitten her, and touched it gently. "The skin isn't broken, thank God." Hawk's hands, too, were trembling a little, and she wondered if it was fear or anger or what.

He was so close. So close. She smelled his aftershave and could see the way the hair grew from his temple. His touch was so very, very gentle. There was a quiet in him that was unlike anything she'd felt from another man. It was easy to imagine him with his horses, taking good care of them, or with a child on his lap.

She wanted to kiss him. So badly. His mouth was shaped so perfectly for it—that lush lower lip, the perfectly carved bow above. His hand moved on her face delicately, and a ripple of aftershocks followed each infinitesimal movement, as if the invisible hairs on her skin were electrically charged just for him.

And it only got worse when he looked up. "Now the other, all right?"

She nodded, trying to keep her breath under control as he pushed the coat open and looked at her breasts. He didn't touch her, but the fact that she knew he was looking at her breasts, at the ravagement of the dress, was almost worse, especially when she realized she wasn't controlling her breath at all, that it was coming in short little rushes, which was making her chest move. "There's a bruise," he said, his voice as thick and dark as original sin.

"Is there?" The words were wispy, nearly lost in the thick atmosphere of the car.

He touched it, very lightly, and Laurie closed her eyes. "Hawk," she whispered. "I—"

"I gotta tell ya, princess," he said, "I'm having a little trouble being a professional here."

"Me, too." She looked at him and very deliberately raised her hand to his face, touching his lips with her fingers. "I don't want you to think I was aroused by that man. I wasn't. Any more than I would have been by somebody stomping on my foot. I'm aroused right now because you are so close and I've been thinking so much about you, and your touch makes me shiver from head to toe."

"I wanted to kill that guy," he said roughly, "I was so jealous it was insane."

"Kiss me, Hawk. Please."

He raised his eyes as he slid his arm around her shoulder to pull her closer, his other hand sliding down from her neck to the expanse of skin showing over her torn dress. He settled his palm across the top of her breasts, and bent in and kissed her.

She made a small sound as their mouths met, gently at first, only lips pressing close, fitting together, hot and tender, so piercing it sent a pain straight through her heart.

He kissed her slowly, thoroughly exploring and teasing, first softly, then with an intent that brought with it a rush of breath. He pulled her tighter with the crook of his elbow, and the hand that rested on her chest shifted just a little, sliding back and forth. Laurie opened her mouth to him, and he accepted the invitation, his tongue swirling into her, inviting her to dance with him in the oldest expression of man and woman.

Laurie lifted unsteady hands to his face, reveling in the pleasurable feel of the strong bones beneath her fingers. She touched his jaw and temple and neck, kissing and kissing and kissing, wanting his hand to do more than rest safely above her bodice. Their kisses grew more intense, more urgent, punctuated with dark rumbles from Hawk, soft gasps from Laurie as they caught their breath in tiny gulps. She found herself pressed against the limo seat, his body warm against her.

And there was, suddenly, a powerful shift of energy between them. It came in the restrained urgency she felt in him, all at once surging through his body and his lips. It was an urgency that was both thrilling and terrifying, filled with such a depth of hunger that she fleetingly wondered how anyone could possibly satisfy such a level of starvation. The hand that had been on her breasts suddenly caught her face, and he kissed her mouth, her chin, her throat. Then her lips again— in an openmouthed, thrusting, agonizingly deep kiss. Laurie responded in kind. She was not herself entirely, but transformed into pure thrumming energy, part of him and herself and the world.

Abruptly, he raised his head, and Laurie saw more in his troubled gaze than he would have liked her knowing: bewilderment and passion and a broken heart that was still bleeding as if an artery had been cut. His breathing was heavy, as was hers, and she simply raised a hand to his face. "It's all right, Hawk," she said quietly.

"Nothing is ever all right," he said. But he didn't pull away. "This is a bad idea for both of us."

She nodded. "Not very professional."

That drew a faint smile, and he swallowed, touched her lip with one finger, then slid his hand down to cover her breasts again. "You've been driving me crazy for days, and now it's gonna be worse." He straightened, pulling her up with him. "But let's not do this, Laurie."

She realized she felt no surprise at his words, and only looked at him as he tucked his coat around her gently, smoothed her hair.

"It'll make it too hard for you to do your job," he said all too earnestly, "and for me to do mine. Maybe when it's all over, we can see where it goes, huh?"

She nodded. "That's wise."

But she knew they wouldn't do anything about this

after the assignment was over. By morning, he'd be terrified at what he had revealed to her here, and he'd erect a wall against her.

And maybe that was best. He needed a different kind of woman. Someone who would know how to reach in and put her hand on all those wounds and staunch the bleeding, someone who could heal him. She accepted his offering for what it was, a way for both of them to regain their dignity. "Who knows what will happen between now and then." Forcing a smile, she said, "I might entirely loathe you."

"Yeah," he said, and cloaked himself in distance, looking out the window to things she couldn't see.

Chapter 9

News of the assault on the princess had evidently hit the local agencies, because there was a circus awaiting them at the hotel.

Laurie saw them from a block away, and ironically, the long limo had trouble navigating the narrow street amid the traffic. This time, she could tell it was far beyond the little knot of paparazzi who'd been following them; there were three news vans—two from major networks, a third independent—and a crowd of journalists and photographers. Her heart sank and Hawk swore. He picked up the limo phone and punched in a number, and at the same time buzzed the driver. "Don't stop," he said. "Just keep moving. And make sure the doors are locked."

Laurie felt raw and overwrought. What she really wanted was a nice glass of wine, a hot bath and no contact with anyone for at least six hours.

Which made her feel miserable about her ability to

do this job. She only half listened as Hawk barked questions about procedure to whoever it was on the other end of the line. Evidently, they wouldn't be returning to the hotel just now. Which meant all her stuff, all the little things that would have helped soothe her, would be left behind, and she wouldn't have them until tomorrow.

She thought about some of the women agents she knew. Would they be smooching with a male partner in the back of a limo? No way. They'd slug anyone who even suggested it. Would they be shaky and frightened after a brief mauling by a man who'd been taken into custody three seconds later? Not a chance.

Hawk hung up the phone. "We're flying out tonight. I guess they were going to make the change, anyway. Bad weather on the way for Dallas—might not get out if we wait for morning."

It wouldn't be so bad to sleep on the plane, Laurie supposed. At least there wouldn't be any press. "I don't know how Princess Julia stands these crowds of media all the time."

"It would be a pain, all right."

She nodded.

He touched her arm. "You okay?"

"Yes." She straightened. "I'm fine." But her heart pounded as the limo moved through the thickest part of the crowd and reporters pounded on the window, yelling questions. She reared away bumping into Hawk's arm. He steadied her, then dropped his hand hastily.

Laurie said, "I hate that I'm not going to have my things on the plane, though." She gave him a rueful smile. "Even when I travel as myself, I carry a small bag with underwear and a fresh blouse in case the luggage gets lost.''

"It'll be there in the morning. We'll have some supper and rest, and get to the hotel in time to get a good night's sleep." He looked at his watch. "Maybe we'll have some intelligence on the perp by then, too."

"This convinces me that it's not Kamal behind all of this," she said, narrowing her eyes.

"What makes you so sure?"

"The princess is carrying the heir to his throne. He might want to capture her for insurance purposes, but he'd order her to be treated with kid gloves. Anyone who manhandled the mother of a sheik like that man did me would be severely and swiftly punished."

Hawk's jaw went hard. "Makes sense." He sighed. "Which means that we *are* dealing with terrorists of some sort, a call you made early on. And it makes this about a thousand times more dangerous."

The danger was a lot more real to Laurie now. She nodded thoughtfully. "There must be some way to draw them out, a subtle taunt or arrangement or something. Or maybe—" she looked up at him "—the incident tonight will end it."

"Not a chance. If it is terrorists, they've already set two bombs and made a few serious bids to kidnap the princess. They're not going to give up."

"The trick is to figure out which terrorists and what they want. Why the princess? Why Montebello? What do they hope to gain? Are they Arab extremists, or a rebel group, maybe? Is it political? Religious? An old feud? Those are the questions we have to find the answers to."

Hawk stroked his chin in a thoughtful gesture. "I'll

see if I can get my father on the phone when we get to New York." From a pocket inside his tux, he took a narrow notebook and scribbled briefly. "Probably want to use a secure phone line, too."

Laurie sank back against the leather seat. "Good idea." She closed her eyes, willing it all to recede. Nothing could be done about any of it right this second. As she started to doze, she remembered she wanted to ask about Caleb Stone. "What's your father's connection to the Sebastianis, anyway? Does he work for them?"

"Not exactly. I'm not sure what he does, to tell you the truth, but he did tell me that he'd fought against the rebels in Montebello when the king was young."

"How intriguing." She inclined her head. "That must have been when you were a child. You didn't live with him?"

"No. He thought it was better if I lived with my mother's relatives on the reservation—and it was, in the end. Hard to get a sense of who you are without those connections. I'm glad in the long run."

But in his voice she heard faint echoes of the boy he'd been, of his yearning to be with his father. "What does he do?"

A faint, puzzled smile crossed his mouth. "You know, I've been thinking lately that he might be a real live mercenary."

Laurie laughed. "Cool, dude."

"Yeah." He rubbed his hands together mockingly. "Wait'll I get home and tell the guys."

The plane was waiting when they arrived at the airport a half hour later. Hawk was relieved to see

that although a few journalists had been alerted to the
change of plan, and clustered beyond a fence, they
were far enough from the runway that even their
shouted questions were indistinct. Laurie ignored
them, safe behind the dark glasses and his tuxedo
coat. Once on the plane, she curled up on the sofa
with a cup of tea Francesco brought to her, a glossy
magazine and a fluffy blanket, effectively shutting out
the world.

"Maybe you should go lie down," Hawk suggested. "Really sleep?"

She shook her head. "I'm a little keyed up. If I lie
down and want to sleep, I won't. If I pretend I'm
going to read here on the couch, I'll sleep like a baby.
You can have the bed if you want it."

"No, I'm good, thanks." Although he really
wanted her out of his line of sight, keyed up didn't
come anywhere close to capturing his mood. He felt
like a caged cat, restless and agitated. Loosening his
tie, he sorted through the music selections, found
some mellow jazz he hoped might ease his tension,
and put on the headphones. He'd leave her alone to
get some rest.

It helped, at least a little. Francesco served a hot
meal of beef tips in some kind of wine sauce, along
with a hearty bread. Hawk ate every bite of his and
had seconds, but Laurie only picked at hers. Then she
settled on the couch more comfortably, took the pins
out of her hair and promptly fell asleep.

Which left Hawk with nothing to do, thousands of
feet above the earth, but look at her. She was very,
very beautiful in the soft lamplight. Her wavy dark
hair was scattered over the pillow in glittery strands,
and her skin was as smooth and white as a bowl of

milk. Without a single freckle or blemish; as poreless
as a length of satin. He liked her nose—aristocrati-
cally shaped, with elegantly flaring nostrils. And her
mouth, which was sexy and full and pouty even without the cut she'd endured.

A ripple of rage moved through him as he looked
at the tender red mark making her lower lip swell a
bit. The blanket was over her shoulder, so he couldn't
see the bruise on her right breast, but the exact pattern
of fingers was burned into his brain—red marks on
tender flesh. Flesh so soft he thought he would die of
the feeling. He had not trusted himself to do more
than just rest his palm across the gentle swells, yet
hours later, an imprint of the contours of her upper
chest lingered clearly.

A twist of shame burned in his gut. Some hero he
turned out to be. Instead of putting his arms around
her, offering comfort when he saw how shaken she
was, he'd surrendered completely to his desire for her,
to his need to possess her mouth, her tongue, her
body. He'd only intended to take a small, sweet taste,
indulge a little of his wish to touch her.

He groaned softly in memory of the erotic picture:
the dress torn to reveal breasts clasped in a shimmery,
elegant undergarment that propped her up like an offering. He'd been able to just make out the nipples
beneath the fabric, pearling as he looked at her, the
flesh rising and falling with her hurried breath, her
lips parting expectantly—

He swore. No excuse for it. None. And even less
for the way he'd lost his head once he started, falling
into some dream he had trouble pulling out of. She
was so eager and tender, so naive and yet so seductive. She wanted him as much as he wanted her, and

it was so tempting to give her the long, slow, explosive sex he sensed she'd never experienced.

But at what cost? Her broken heart at the very least, because she wasn't the kind of woman who'd keep love and sex separated. Worse than that, though, was the possibility that his own emotions were getting too tangled up in her. In this job he couldn't afford to have his instincts diluted. Bottom line was that Hawk was the only thing standing between her and the terrorists.

Terrorists who were not of a humane mindset. If one would maul her in public, what would two or three do in private? The idea made him sick.

Whatever happened, he had to keep her safe. From here on out, he was the boss—and he didn't care if she liked it or not.

She shifted on the couch, rolling over to her back. The blanket stayed with her for the most part, but one long leg slipped out, the ankle graceful, the thigh slim. He closed his eyes. *Don't look. Don't think. Don't want.*

The day had been a long one, and the constant travel was catching up with him. To his surprise, Hawk found he could sleep after all, and as he drifted off, surrounded by the sweet jazz of Miles Davis, he realized he hadn't had time to brood about his sorrows all day. Interesting.

It was three in the morning before they got to the hotel. Laurie, having slept very well for nearly five hours on the plane, discovered she was not particularly tired. The room was predictably elegant and perfect, with fresh flowers and marble sinks and a view of Central Park, and it made her smile to realize how fast a person got used to luxury.

Hawk had slept on the plane, too, and picked up the remote control to turn on the news. "Do you mind? I'm not sure I'm ready to go to bed right this minute."

"Not at all. I think I'll shower. And then, if you don't mind, I'd like to watch the videos of the princess again—oh, heck. I don't have those, either." She sighed. "I'm getting a little tired of being in one hotel room after another, aren't you?"

"Yeah. They don't really offer much in the way of entertainment. You want me to see if there's a movie we can agree on?"

"That's a good idea. I'll just shower and be back in a few minutes."

Laurie thought she'd put the incident at the gala in perspective. Sleep always made things look less dramatic, but she still felt a little queasy when she took off Hawk's jacket and saw the damage that had been inflicted. The dress was in tatters across the bodice, the delicate, loosely woven fabric having shredded after the first brutal tear. What a shame, she thought. The dress had probably cost more than her monthly salary. She took it off and left it in a pile on the floor. Maybe some lucky maid could do something with that skirt.

She turned the water on hot, stripped off her stockings, bra and underwear and made herself look in the mirror. The imprint of a man's fingers showed clearly across her breast. Her lower lip was swollen, and the black eye was even more visible now that her makeup had worn off. She looked like she'd been brawling.

And in a way, she supposed she had. The idea

made her smile. She was trained to manage the brawling, and in fact, she'd kept the princess safe today, hadn't she?

She grinned at the reflection disappearing behind the steam, feeling empowered. Her body looked good to her, strong and healthy and sexy. She even thought of the kissing in the limo with Hawk and rationalized that it was fairly normal. A healthy response to danger.

And probably best left behind.

A flicker of the taste of him crossed her mouth. The memory of his need rippled through her body. She'd had no idea until that moment just how lost he was. No wonder his father had hauled him out of his seclusion to take this job. It was good for a man to stay busy, keep his demons at bay. She'd learned that lesson very well at the age of twelve after the tornado, and it was one you didn't forget.

She found herself singing as she showered, washed her hair, scrubbed away the disturbing residue and emotion left from the assault. The hotel, alerted to the fact that they had no bags, had sent toothbrushes, combs and other toiletries to tide them over, and she loved them for it. When she was finished, she dried her hair and left it wild on her shoulders, put the heavy white robe on and went out to see what Hawk had found on television.

He was watching CNN, a story about a missing child. "What do you get out of that?" she asked, plopping down in a chair.

"What do you mean?"

"Watching the news. I mean, everybody probably needs the headlines—we want to know if there's a war or who won an election or if there are big storms on the way. But what good does it do us to hear about murdered spouses and missing children and all the other tragedies that happen around the world every minute?''

His mouth turned down at the corners. ''I don't know,'' he said slowly. ''I can't say that I ever thought about it before.''

''Maybe you should.''

''Maybe. But turning it off doesn't make it go away.''

''But what can you do about any of it?''

''Nothing, I guess. Maybe knowing helps spread the burden, helps keep people aware of the dangers.''

''No, you know what I think?'' She sat up and reached for an orange in a basket on the coffee table, talking as she peeled it. ''I think it just makes people worry. My dad? He's a champion worrier. He worries about everything. Who's gonna get cancer, what storm might take everything, who might have an accident—it's like his religion to fret. He keeps a scanner in the living room and hears all the fire and police calls in the entire county—and it just drives me nuts. I mean, yeah, people are having heart attacks, falling down and breaking their skulls, getting into accidents, getting shot, getting hurt, getting sick every single minute of every single day.'' She bit into a section of orange. ''All it does is make him worry more, about things he's never even realized he should worry about.''

Unexpectedly, Hawk chuckled. ''I know people like that. Fretters. Even people who keep scanners.''

''It's the same thing, watching all the bad news all the time. Read the headlines in the newspaper every morning and trust me, you won't miss much.'' She offered him a section of orange and he shook his head politely. "If something big happens, like an invasion, you can get all the detail you need in five minutes flat."

He lifted one eyebrow and clicked through the stations until he got to one playing music videos. "Better?"

"Much."

"How'd you end up with such a healthy attitude, Laurie? You're so cheerful all the time. And I don't mean that in a bad way. It's admirable. How is it possible to be so friendly and hardworking and upbeat all the time?"

"I don't know," Laurie said. "I guess nothing really bad has ever happened to me."

"That's impossible. You're what? Twenty-five, twenty-six? Everybody has something happen by that age."

"Twenty-seven, and no, I haven't. Just normal life." She leaned back and propped her bare feet on the coffee table, careful that her robe was tucked around her. "You lost your mom when you were young and you've had to deal with this other big loss now, a really violent scene. That kinda sticks with you."

Her words must have struck a nerve, because he bowed his head, hiding his eyes. "I guess."

"What happened to the boy, Hawk? I wanted to ask last night."

"He went to his grandmother, his mother's mother." His voice grew a little rough. "It was good for both of them. A way to get through the loss."

"And it's a better place for him than his home was?"

He gave a humorless laugh. "Wouldn't take much to beat that."

"Maybe that's what you need to think about when this comes up. Not about your partner and the crime scene, but about the boy, who is safe now."

Hawk raised his eyes, and they were suspiciously bright. Not with tears, but as close as a man like him could ever get. "Believe it or not, nobody has said that before. It might really help." His jaw worked. "Thank you."

She grinned. "Just call me Dr. Laurie." She popped a slice of orange in her mouth and laughed at her play on the famous radio talk show host's name.

His eyes crinkled deeply with his grin. "That was bad."

"Oh, I can get lots worse than that."

He stood. "Listen, honey, don't take this the wrong way, but I'm going to go to bed now."

"Oh." She was disappointed. Wide-awake, feeling good, she didn't want to be alone. "Okay. I'll see you in the morning."

He paused beside the chair and put his hand on her shoulder. "The trouble is, you see, that I know you're naked beneath that robe, and I'm just not all that strong."

She grinned up at him. "Ah! Okay, you weakling. Off to bed with you, then. I'll just sit out here by myself and be bored."

For a minute, he wavered. She saw the gleam in his eyes, the slow heat of yearning cross his mouth, then he patted her shoulder firmly and left her.

Probably for the best, Laurie told herself, taking control of the remote.

Probably.

Chapter 10

Laurie slept a bit, but was awake and refreshed by nine the following morning. Their bags had been delivered toward dawn, and Laurie gratefully changed into her own clothes, somehow needing the reassurance of a pair of jeans and a sweatshirt. A reminder of who she was, she supposed. It was a little disorienting to think constantly as someone else.

They would spend the day in New York, waiting for the dinner this evening. It was a different sort of appearance than Laurie had previously handled—not, she thought with a scowl, that she'd really been all that brilliant thus far—a meeting with several business leaders who were concerned about their investments in Montebello. The princess had often performed such duties for her father in the past; she was not only beautiful, but blessed with both a canny sense of diplomacy and a business acumen that had served her family very well. Laurie had reviewed the material provided to her by the princess, the king and the FBI, but she still felt a little nervous about it.

And the idea of hanging around the hotel all day with no one but the devastatingly delicious Hawk was intolerable. "I need a workout," she said as he emerged, looking tousled and all the more overwhelming because of it. "Can you set it up? A hotel this size must have a gym."

"I'm sure it does." He picked up the phone. "What's your pleasure, princess? Swimming? Treadmill? Weights?"

"Treadmill," she said. "Stairstepper if they have it." The more vigorous the workout, the better.

He spoke into the phone and hung up. "They asked that you give them an hour."

She rolled her eyes. "Fine."

He poured coffee and chuckled. "What's wrong with you, Miss Sun and Smiles? Reading too many newspapers? Listening to the news?"

"No. This is just really boring. I'm not used to sitting around with nothing to do for hours on end."

"Welcome to the downside of the job. It's ninety percent boring, ten percent excitement."

She sighed. "Easy for you to say. You can wander all over New York if you want to." She gestured irritably toward the window, where, far below, rivers of cars poured through tall canyons of buildings. "I've never been to New York. I'd love to get out."

"I can understand that. I've never been here, either." He looked out the window with a pensive expression. "Well, what would Julia do here for fun?"

"I'm not sure."

He looked...mischievous this morning. Well

rested, his eyes glittering with anticipation. "Maybe she'd go shopping."

Laurie brightened. "Maybe she would. Would her bodyguard go with her?"

"Sure. Along with an army of guys in black suits and dark glasses and little speakers in their ears." He made a sound like crackling electronics.

"Oh." Her spirits sank. "If it would require extra manpower, they won't approve it." She gave an exaggerated frown. "Too bad. I was thinking of Tiffany's or Cartier's or something. It would have been fun to pretend." With a sigh, she added, "I don't know how celebrities do it. It would drive me nuts."

"I know how they do it." Hawk grinned suddenly, eyes twinkling. "I'll have to get approval, but I have an idea."

She inclined her head. "You're so different this morning. What changed?"

He met her eyes. "I don't know, Laurie. Maybe you're just a good influence on me."

"Oh. Well, good."

"Give me a half hour. Have some breakfast. Oh, and let me cancel the clearing of the weight room, huh?"

She laughed. "Good idea."

Hawk had spent a lot of time in the service guarding dignitaries and heads of state, and one of the problems was the children of such luminaries, especially older teens who were not at all interested in boring dinners or any of the other things their parents did. Kids the world over wanted *out,* and he'd learned from the experts how to make it happen.

He dialed headquarters from a pay phone and received approval for his plan. There was little information from the man they'd apprehended the night before; unlike those involved in the bombings, this one was a professional—at keeping his mouth shut, in any case—and had given them nothing to go on. In terms of progress on the case, the FBI were exactly where they had been yesterday.

It bothered Hawk. He'd dropped the ball last night, and as a result, Laurie had nearly been kidnapped.

Or maybe not. He had to admit she'd handled the situation quite well. Maybe he needed to let go a little, trust her.

And maybe... The thought crept in, seeming so perfectly obvious. Maybe he could trust himself, too. Trust that he was a good cop, that he had good instincts and could protect one woman pretty well.

It was an odd feeling. He hadn't trusted anything in a long time.

Whistling softly, he sought out the concierge and recruited his help with both a list of supplies and a way to keep reporters in the dark. Most of what Hawk needed was available within a four block area—it was New York, after all. He bought a curly blond wig and bright lipstick at a beauty supply store, a couple of shirts and some tennis shoes at a department store, a couple of hats in a souvenir store. He walked back to the hotel with his finds, pleased at his cleverness.

"Well, princess," he said, carrying his bags into the suite. Laurie was sitting by the window, looking with longing toward the street scene below. "I think we've got a plan."

She jumped up to examine his finds, and laughed as she pulled them out of the bags. "Oh, this is great!" she cried. "I'll be right back."

She emerged fifteen minutes later in an oversize baseball shirt and red hightop tennis shoes. The long, curly wig she'd pulled back with a scrunchy, fastened halfway down her back. The baseball hat she'd turned backward, and her lips were a bright, cherry red. She looked about sixteen, tops. "What d'you think?"

"Perfect." Since his picture had been taken so much with her, Hawk had picked up some props for himself. He'd tucked his hair up under a baseball cap and put on a pair of horn-rimmed prescriptionless glasses and—he'd been quite pleased with himself over this touch—a pair of overalls.

She hooted. "Where are we from, Mr. Hicksville?"

"Nebraska."

She laughed. "You rat. I definitely need gum for this," she said, admiring herself. "Bubble gum."

"Are you ready? Let's see the sights."

They were hustled down the back stairs and let out in the alley. Hawk took her hand and they dashed to the sidewalk, emerging into a brilliantly sunny day alive with the noises of the city. For a minute, holding hands, they stood there grinning at each other, surrounded by the hooting of horns and the sound of engines and the clatter of the subway beneath their feet.

Laurie grinned up at him with red, red lips, and her eyes sparkled. "This is so great, Hawk. Thank you."

He squeezed her hand. "Let's go find a map."

"No," she said, "let's not. We'll just ask people. Talk to them."

Infected by the sunlight, by the freshness of her face, the excitement in her eyes, Hawk felt a swell of perfect contentment. "Okay." He took her hand and

pulled her along, liking the fantasy that they were just
a pair of young tourists, wide-eyed and thrilled to be
in the Big Apple, free from all care. It could almost
be true.

They got directions to Fifth Avenue from a bagel
shop, where they picked out giant, fresh bagels and
smeared them with cream cheese. Then they walked
up that famous avenue window-shopping, craning
their necks to look up at the buildings. Laurie was
embarrassed at first. "Aren't we supposed to act cool
and not do that?"

"What fun is it being cool?"

She had to agree that he had a point. So she let
herself stare all she wanted, fascinated by glimpses of
little gardens on the tops of buildings and hints of
secret hideaways. Over and over, Hawk took her
hand, and it was somehow right to walk with him that
way; they could tell themselves it was because they
were acting the part of two young lovers in the city
for kicks, so there wasn't even any danger in it.

They walked the sidewalks beneath tall trees at the
edge of Central Park, watching mothers with strollers
and kids on skates and old men on bikes. They
stopped to examine a tableful of used books and one
of miniatures painted by a Rastafarian in a striped,
knitted hat. Through the trees, they glimpsed some
cages and Hawk asked, "Do you want to go to the
zoo?"

"Not really, unless you're just dying to go. I always get kind of sad over animals in cages."

"Somehow," he said, "that doesn't surprise me."

"Don't you always think of what they might be
like in a jungle or on a mountain, wherever they were

supposed to live?'' His fingers were laced with hers, solid and warm. ''It's like...slavery or something.''

They were passing a big old tree, and he stopped. ''You know, that's the kind of thing you say that keeps making me want to kiss you.''

She looked up at him, smiling at the horn-rimmed glasses that obscured but didn't completely hide his beautiful eyes. ''I think that, between us, kissing is a fairly dangerous act.''

He moved his fingers, working them tighter between hers. ''That's true.'' He looked away. ''How about the museum, then? Want to go inside?''

Laurie looked at the monolithic structure, the imposing columns and the banners proclaiming a new exhibit. Enormous numbers of people milled around the steps, and she shook her head. ''I don't think I want to go inside anywhere. Let's just keep walking, see what we see. Do you mind?''

''No,'' he said. ''Not at all.''

In curious harmony, they walked the streets of New York. Laurie let everything go, just enjoying his company. And enjoy it she did. He bought silly hats and souvenirs, postcards to send to his aunts and uncles and cousins; he stopped at a hot dog vendor and bought them foot-longs with mustard. She wandered beside him, intrigued when he couldn't pass up a used-books store, then surprised by the aisles that captured him: forensics and crime studies, but also butterflies and history and essays. One battered edition with a water-stained cover and a sticker that said ''50 cents'' made him chortle softly.

''Oh, man,'' he said, showing it to her. ''Have you ever read this guy?''

The title of the book was *Late Night Thoughts Lis-*

tening to Mahler's Ninth Symphony. The author was
Lewis Thomas. "Looks deep," Laurie said.

"I guess," Hawk said, flipping it open. "He's a
scientist, or was—I think he died. He writes about
music and science and nature and humanity. Beautiful
stuff."

His head was bent, showing the swirl of dark hair
from his nape that was swept up under his hat, leaving
his neck bare. For some reason, that detail, together
with his genuine excitement over a book of essays,
stung her hard. With his long fingers, he flipped
through the pages, and read aloud, unselfconsciously,
in that wonderfully melodic voice of his. Laurie
barely heard the words, she was so stricken with a
realization.

It was going to kill her to leave him behind.

When he raised his head, though, she managed to
smile brightly. "Beautiful."

He bought the book and they wandered on again.
When they passed a dark, narrow little place, sup-
posedly an antique store but in reality a junkshop, she
was the one who pulled him inside. The store smelled
of mildew. An old woman sat behind the counter, her
nose the biggest thing about her. "Hello, hello," she
said in an Eastern European accent. "Come, look
around. I have many beautiful things."

And in spite of the dinginess of the building, Laurie
discovered it was true. The treasures were clean and
neatly arranged on tables. She was charmed by a set
of carved bells, an elaborate tabletop fountain depict-
ing a forest and elfish creatures, and a beautiful red
silk scarf, embroidered delicately with gold thread in
a paisley pattern around the edges. She decided to buy
the scarf, knowing even as she did so that it was her

memento of the day. That sometime in the future she would take it out of her drawer and think of Hawk.

In a corner, she found an enormous collection of dolls. Most of them were baby dolls—old ones, with wild hair and plastic legs scarred by a lot of dragging and banging. "Oh, this always makes me sad," she said, picking one of them up. "Abandoned toys." The doll still talked, and bleated out a "Ma-ma" when Laurie held her up. Nearly all of her hair was gone, and she wore no shoes, just a little blue dress that was ragged around the bottom. "But somebody loved this doll pretty well, once upon a time."

Hawk picked up a GI Joe wearing only his trousers, and bopped the baby on the head with it. "C'mon, baby, let's fight."

Laurie tsked and rolled her eyes, pulling the doll into a safety zone against her shoulder. "What is it with guys? Always mean to dolls."

He made a kissing noise and held it to her face. "Joey wants you, honey."

She laughed, and spied on the table a Barbie in a flowered dress. "Oh, look!" she cried. "I had this very doll. Mine probably still lives in my mom's attic. She never throws anything away." This one was in decent shape, and Laurie adjusted the legs, recalling another day a long time ago. "Remember I told you about the tornado? Well, I think I also told you I was hiding from my brothers. I had all my dolls up there in a secret hiding place, because they always did things like put Magic Marker mustaches on them and stuff. Tornado took 'em that time." She smoothed the Barbie's coppery hair. "Three weeks later, we found all of them in the back of a pickup truck four miles away. They were standing in a little line against the tire well, like somebody had placed them there.'' She put the doll down. ''Only one of them was upside down.''

''Amazing,'' Hawk said. ''It seems like it would tear them to pieces.''

''You'd think so. That's how it is with tornadoes, though. You just never know.'' She frowned meditatively, carrying the red scarf to the counter. ''I guess it's kind of miraculous.''

''I would say so. I think I'd like to see one someday.''

She rolled her eyes. ''Only the uninitiated ever say that.''

When they emerged, Laurie realized with a jolt that the sun was more than halfway down the western slope of sky. ''I guess we have to get back now, don't we?'' she said.

''I'm afraid so. Cab or bus?''

She grinned at him, loving that it was even a question he could ask. ''Oh, let's have one more adventure and catch a bus.''

''My thoughts exactly.'' He suddenly looped an arm around her neck. It was playful at first, the kind of thing a guy did to another guy, a wrestling hold. ''It was a good day, wasn't it?''

''Yes,'' Laurie said, looking up at him. He pulled her a little closer, trapping her head in the crook of his elbow. Their bodies connected at the torso, and Laurie tried not to notice. ''You're kind of fun when you stop brooding.''

He just looked down at her, his mouth only inches away, and Laurie wanted, so much, to kiss him. The sun gilded his eyelashes, swooped over his brow. ''I forgot how it could be, just hanging out.''

She resisted the urge to nestle closer, but she couldn't keep herself from spreading her fingers on his waist, couldn't stop looking at his mouth. "Maybe just one kiss would be okay," she said quietly. "Out here in public and all."

"I really thought you'd never ask," he said, and bent his head with a soft sound of relief.

It should have been safe, in the street, with people walking by. Someone, really, should have bumped them.

Instead, the instant their lips touched, it was like an explosion. Laurie felt herself ignite—all of her, from head to toes—and at the same time go soft. She felt his body turn into hers, felt his arm go around her, and all the time they were kissing, deeply, hungrily. Laurie reveled in the details—the tip of his nose brushing her cheek, the sense of his jaw and his chest, the taste of his tongue, which was not sweet, but somehow exotic, redolent of the way pine smelled.

It felt much too long and much too short all at once. A few seconds in real time, probably, she thought vaguely as they mutually pulled apart, eyes meeting. The air smelled of a strange combination of baking bread, exhaust and the heat of his skin coming through his shirt. Laurie wanted to stay right in this moment, looking up into his beautiful green eyes, for the rest of time.

"Thank you for such a great day," she said.

He grinned, looking youthful and unconcerned. "No, thank *you.*" A bus was trundling down the street and they moved toward the curb. When it stopped, Hawk checked with the driver to make sure it would take them back, then pulled her behind him up the steps. They found seats midway down the aisle, settling on the narrow bench in a deliciously close fit. Laurie loved the feeling of his thigh next to hers, loved the smell of him—sunlight and moss. Loved the way he took her hand and just held it in his own. "Do you mind?"

"No."

In front of them was an older man in a brown-checkered shirt. Tufts of gray hair sprang out from beneath his hat. Next to him was a little girl, maybe six or so, who turned around to stare at Hawk and Laurie. She had enormous dark eyes, and her tiny fingernails were painted yellow. "Hi. My grandpa took me to feed the ducks. What did you do?"

Her grandfather touched her back. "Don't be rude, Misha."

"Oh, it's all right," Laurie said. "We are not as lucky as you. We don't live here and we just went to see your wonderful city."

"It *is* a wonderful city," the child said with great maturity. "You should come at Christmas and go skating."

"We'll remember that."

And Laurie glanced up at Hawk, suddenly sad. He gazed down at her, looking just as stricken as she felt. Their fingers twined more tightly.

Oh, dear, Laurie thought. She was really falling in love. And there wasn't anything she could do to escape it.

Chapter 11

Back at the hotel, they separated to get ready for the dinner, and as Hawk showered, he told himself to pull himself together. Get real. Figure out how bad this was for both of them. He listed the reasons: he was a wreck emotionally and she deserved something a lot better than that. They were caught in the unreal world of undercover work. They were partners and shouldn't be getting emotionally involved.

But even as he told himself these things, as he patted cologne on his jaw and examined his fingernails to make sure they were well and truly clean, he was whistling under his breath. The darkness that had clouded every thought, every dream and waking moment, every movement of his days and nights for nearly a year, was diminishing. In its place he was beginning to feel light and clean, as if he were made of sunlight. Yellow sunlight.

The analytical side of him kept tossing out objections: this new emotion was false. It was a reaction to the circumstances, to getting away from his real life. It wouldn't last. He would, in the end, have his heart broken, or she'd get hers ripped in half and they'd both be in a worse place than before. In the end, it wouldn't be something gilded and fresh, but a painful memory, the lost promise of something sweet. It was always that way.

Even to his own internal ears, his thoughts sounded cynical, but he had good reason for cynicism. His parents' thwarted love affair was example enough by itself, and he'd seen over and over that love didn't last, didn't stay true, couldn't survive the turmoil life inflicted. It was sad, but it was reality. Better, in the long run, to just avoid deep entanglements, anything that would hurt that much.

But the relentlessly bright idea that had infected him—a virus he'd caught from Laurie, he thought with a smile—was the possibility that it didn't have to work out like that. Why couldn't they have found something good here? Unexpectedly, and purely by accident, but something good nonetheless?

Why not something good instead of something bad for once?

He was actually pretty hungry, and although Laurie would be having dinner with a select group of corporate leaders who wanted reassurance that the trouble in Montebello would not affect their business interests, he didn't know what arrangements would be made for a mere bodyguard. He'd learned that it took Laurie a good hour or better to get herself into the part, so he called the kitchen to have them bring him a sandwich. After the long, enjoyable day in the sun, he really wanted a beer, too, but he had a job to do tonight. Later, if he still wanted it, he could order beer.

After he ordered, he used the house phone to leave a message on his father's pager. A few minutes later, the cell phone rang, and Hawk picked it up. "Hey, old man. How you doing?"

"Not bad. You sound good." In his father's dulcet tones, Hawk heard a smile. "Everything going well?"

He glanced over his shoulder at the closed door. "Very well. Anything on the guy we took into custody last night?"

"Nothing." The older man sighed. "He's a professional. Won't crack, I'm sure. We've been working with the senator who threw the party, and with the planners, but so far that hasn't turned up anything, either."

A ripple of unease touched Hawk. "Any more threats?"

"No. But be alert. The whole world saw what happened last night—it's in all the tabloids—and although this business dinner tonight isn't all that public, anyone in the know would have access to the information. We've slated extra guards for the restaurant, and the car will be escorted. You're also flying out to L.A. tonight instead of waiting until morning."

A piercing thorn of disappointment stuck in Hawk's chest, and he realized he'd been very seriously considering something else for this night. Long, lazy, hot sex with a woman who'd been painting his world in colors of sunlight and cherry-red.

His bright mood evaporated in an instant. "Why?"

"There is some concern that the hotel is not secure enough."

"Damn." He thought of the risks he'd taken today,

trusting that the net of FBI would keep them—keep Laurie—safe. And again, more forcefully, he swore.

"We've named a special team to transport your bags and stick with the plane, just to be safe, and they'll be flying with you from here on out. The last stop is L.A., and then you'll go to the family home in Aspen. If our terrorists haven't made a move by then, you'll have to lure them out." Caleb paused. "You'll have to let her be taken, if necessary, James."

Hawk's gut clenched, and he recognized what his father was telling him. It might have been better if Laurie had let herself be carried off last night—but she'd been surprised, as he had been, and neither of their reactions had been what the operation needed. "I understand," he said gruffly.

"She can do it, Son."

"Yeah, I know." She emerged then, in a cloud of the princess's perfume, and Hawk felt another emotion entirely slam into him. "I gotta go, Dad," he said, and hung up without waiting to hear if there was anything else, his senses were so completely snared by the vision in front of him.

Laurie saw him staring and paused a little uncertainly. "Is it okay?" She touched her face. "Is the makeup covering the bruises?"

"Yeah," he managed to answer. The dress, deep gold with a glittery overlay, was very simply cut, with straight, close lines that hinted at the curves beneath. But the glittery part shone in the most subtle way, illuminating the shape of her breasts and the small swell of her lower belly and the front of her thighs. Straps the width of thread held it up, and he couldn't help thinking what it would be like to see them break.

"You don't even want to know what I'm thinking," he said ruefully, and smiled. "Whew."

She touched her hips and adjusted the diaphanous shawl over her shoulders. "It feels a little dangerous, this dress, but Mrs. Watson insisted that this was what the princess would wear. I might feel better in a suit."

"No," he said, thinking of the pictures of the princess he'd seen. She was very aware of her feminine side, and unashamed of it. "American women wear suits to business dinners. The princess is smarter than that."

Laurie took a breath. "Okay, whatever you say."

A knock came at the door, and Hawk was glad of the distraction. "That's my sandwich," he said.

"Oh, you're a rat."

He wiggled his eyebrows. "A smart rat." He collected the sandwich, tipped the waiter and closed the door. "We need to get out of here in a few minutes, but I'm warning you now that we're spending the night on the plane. They want us out of the hotel."

She showed no reaction for a moment, her body very still, and he wondered if she'd been hoping for a different scenario, too. With the princess's quiet dignity, she said, "I suppose I'd better put together a few things for the night, then."

Impulsively, Hawk said, "Will you wear the dress on the plane?"

He was watching her reflection, so he saw her swallow before she raised her eyes and met his gaze in the mirror, holding it for a long, long time before she said simply, "Yes."

They held each other's gazes, communicating what they would not say aloud. *Tonight...*

The dinner was agony for Hawk. Security was excellent, as his father had promised—with extra men, dressed as waiters and doormen, posted everywhere. The meal itself was served in an opulent nineteenth-century-style room lit with braces of candles and supplemental lamps. A red Persian carpet covered the floor, baroque music was piped in over hidden speakers and a trio of servers attended the small group exclusively.

Hawk was stationed to one side with a clear view of the door. Laurie sat with her back to the wall, the four businessmen arrayed around her, and he understood Mrs. Watson's insistence on this dress. In the low-lit room, she glowed like a taper, the fabric shining discreetly, her skin luminescent above it.

Apart from security, the only thing he had to occupy himself with through the long, long, meal was watching her, and it was an amazing performance. She used Julia's soft tones to draw the men's attention—a subtlety of command Hawk had often seen in powerful women. Her tone of voice was not at all subservient, but so powerfully dignified that the entire table fell silent to listen.

And it was not only in appearance that she mimicked the princess. She'd done her homework with a thoroughness that impressed him, answering questions and addressing concerns without a moment's hesitation, radiating confidence and supreme certainty that all would be well in Montebello.

As they waited for dessert, one of the men leaned forward. "Your highness, I don't want to intrude on your grief, but there is concern about the line of inheritance if your brother is…if he doesn't…"

Laurie cut in quietly, her expression sober. "If they find his body?"

"Er...yes."

She looked at Hawk across the room, as if drawing strength from him, and he saw her take a deep breath. So did all the other men at the table. Their gazes were fixed somewhere just below her chin. "I have absolute faith that Lucas will be found," she said, and put her hand on her diaphragm. "I feel, here, that he is alive."

Demurely, she lowered her eyes, as if steadying herself. "But if he is not, I assure you that my father will name an appropriate heir."

"Is there any possibility that it will be Rashid Kamal?"

A startled look crossed her face, so real Hawk was sure it wasn't feigned. "None," she said, and the tone was firm enough that no one else broached the subject. Gracefully, they let it go. The servers came in with yet another bottle of wine and trays of delicate desserts, something chocolate with a red syrup. Laurie laughed at a joke one of the men made and bent to taste the chocolate. A fine gold chain glittered around her neck, long enough to just brush the top of her breasts, and Hawk found his libido on overdrive as he imagined what lay ahead for them tonight. He imagined the dress sliding down her long white body, imagined putting his mouth on her neck, imagined tasting her long, long thighs.

His body reminded him that he had a job to do, but before he could tear his gaze away, she glanced up and caught his eye. For a long second, they were alone in the opulent room, and he let his gaze fall, touch her breasts. Most distinctly, her nipples pearled.

He let one side of his mouth lift the tiniest bit, a smile of anticipation.

Laurie thought the meal would never end. Hawk stood to one side of the room, self-contained and elegant in a black suit, his hair pulled back in a severe style that emphasized the high slant of his cheekbones, the clean line of his jaw, his beautiful mouth.

It was hard to believe she'd only known him for such a short time and she'd seen so many sides of him already. She briefly recalled the way he'd looked this afternoon, so earnest and bookish in the horn-rimmed glasses, and the way he'd looked that first night at headquarters, severe and unsmiling. Both were a huge contrast to the elegant and dangerous-looking man who kept watch tonight. A man whose eyes gave away what he was thinking every time he looked at her.

Which made it very difficult for her to concentrate on the task before her, though she managed fairly well. She'd learned at the party in Dallas to give herself a space of time, a few seconds before she answered a query or challenge, and it served her well tonight. As if the princess were standing at her shoulder, whispering answers into her ear, Laurie replied easily and simply, rephrasing questions she did not entirely know how to answer.

And all the while, she kept imagining the dark interior of the limousine on the way to the airport. Imagined Hawk's hands and mouth on her, imagined hers on him.

In all of her life, she'd never burned to touch a man. Not like this. She'd felt curiosity and mild desire, had even enjoyed the act of sex the few times she'd actually indulged, but all of that felt ridiculously transparent now. Every millimeter of her body felt slightly swollen, exaggeratedly alert. The edge of the tablecloth, brushing her knees, felt too rough. The ice in her water glass was colder than the North Pole. The chocolate-and-raspberry truffle exploded against her tongue.

Then it was finally, finally over. Laurie managed to take her leave of the businessmen with grace, feeling Hawk's body just behind hers in a radiant line of heat that nearly made her shudder. Without speaking, he put his hand on the small of her back and they walked to the limo, where two men in dark suits were waiting to open the door for them.

Laurie ducked in, not even minding the popping flashbulbs of the paparazzi this time, anticipating only the moments ahead, finally within reach. Hawk climbed in and sat down beside her, staring straight before him as if she didn't know he was burning with the same heat she was.

But instead of smartly closing the door behind them as they'd done in the past, the two FBI agents climbed into the limo with them. "Special orders," the tall blond one said. "There's been a bomb threat." He held out his hand. "Alex Pachek."

"How do you do?" Laurie said. Her chest felt like it was caving in from disappointment.

"You flying with us to L.A.?" Hawk asked.

"Maybe as far as Aspen," said the other. "I'm David Stroo. You're Caleb's son, right?"

"Call me Hawk."

Laurie turned her face to the window as the car started to move. Next to her, Hawk's body was a painful reminder of what they'd just lost. What she'd

probably lost for good, if she were honest with herself. If he had any time at all to think, the special
world they'd built today would evaporate. He would
begin to pull away.

And then she would lose him.

How long did she have? A few more days? She
watched the kaleidoscopic whirl of lights that was
Manhattan speed by in the darkness, and ached with
missing him before he was even gone. She would
never forget this day. Never.

She didn't speak much as they drove to the airport.
The three men traded stories of various cases, over-
nights and long assignments. She did listen carefully
when they talked about this case, the various bits and
pieces she and Hawk had already worked out and
discussed, but she didn't trust herself to add much.

At the airport, the two agents climbed out first, and
Laurie picked up her purse, waiting for Hawk to get
out after them. Instead, he turned to her silently,
pressed a kiss to his finger and touched her lips.

She kissed it back in promise.

It turned out that Francesco, the regular steward,
had been grounded and taken into custody. The real
princess Julia had protested vehemently, according to
the agents, but some questionable items had shown
up on a routine re-check of all personnel.

Laurie looked troubled. "I would trust Julia's judg-
ment." They were all belted into the luxurious sitting
area of the plane, awaiting clearance for takeoff.
"What was it that made them suspicious?"

"He has a cousin who is affiliated with the Brothers of Darkness, an extremist terrorist organization

that would love to get its hands on the riches in Tamir.''

''A cousin doesn't mean Francesco is a terrorist,'' Laurie protested.

''Why the hell wasn't that information turned up before this?'' Hawk asked. He'd cast off his jacket and tie and now rolled up the sleeves of his plain white shirt.

One of the agents shrugged. ''Slipped through the cracks, obviously. It happens. There're so many terrorist affiliations these days that we have a hard time keeping up with them.''

''What did Kamal have to say about the kidnapping attempt?'' Hawk asked.

''Denied all connection to it.''

''And King Marcus?''

''He's caught between a rock and a hard place, you know?'' The agent spread his hands. ''His big concern is that nothing happens to Julia.''

''No sign of Prince Lucas?'' Laurie asked. She'd felt a strange, painful rush of empathy for the princess when the businessmen had brought up the missing prince.

He gave a slow shake of his head. ''Nor of Rashid.''

Laurie felt a wave of sympathy for the grieving fathers, and for Julia. Her brother likely dead, and her lover missing, too. How terrible! It would be horrible to lose one of her own brothers. ''I hope they find them both, soon.''

''It would sure relieve a lot of pressure in the area.''

The plane geared up for takeoff and the agent

clicked on the remote control VCR and television. "They have anything good here?"

The other agent opened the cabinet. "Lots. *Matrix?*" He looked over his shoulder questioningly at Laurie.

She grinned. "Have at it. As soon as we're airborne, I'm going to bed. It's been a long day." She felt Hawk's gaze, but managed to avoid looking at him. Instead, she gazed out the window as they lifted off and climbed rapidly, the lights of New York receding all too quickly into the anonymous darkness. Visions of the day flashed through her mind—Hawk at Central Park, sitting beside her on the bus, holding her hand. She'd felt such a rich tenderness from him, something she'd never felt from a man before.

After a moment, she couldn't avoid just one small peek at him. She raised her eyes and caught him watching her, his head cocked to one side, a faint smile on his mouth. As soon as their eyes met, they were back in that perfect, quiet world together, a place only the two of them could occupy. He inclined his head ever so slightly toward the bedroom.

She feigned a yawn. The young agents were already enraptured by the movie, and barely noticed when she rose. "I think I'll go read," she said, unbuckling her seat belt. "Good night, gentlemen."

They barely nodded at her. David, the short one, said, "Stop the tape for a second, will you? I want to see if I can find something to eat in there."

"Galley's that way," Hawk said. "I'll show you." To Laurie, he said, "Maybe I'll take the chair in there afterwhile, if you don't mind? I've seen this movie."

"That's fine," she said, and was surprised at how adept she was becoming at this acting business. Her voice hardly held a tremor at all. "Good night, everyone."

Chapter 12

Hawk managed to spend ten minutes with the agents without cracking, but the whole time the thought of Laurie on the other side of that bedroom door, wearing that amazing dress, was pulling on his skin like some invisible magnet. When he saw that they were truly engrossed, he stood up. "Have fun, guys. I'm gonna catch a few winks."

Alex looked up, lifting an eyebrow. "Sure, man," he said with a leer. "Don't do anything I wouldn't do."

Hawk narrowed his eyes. "What's that supposed to mean?"

"She's a babe."

"She's my partner," Hawk countered, his heart sinking. That close.

"Hey, man, whatever." Alex turned his attention back to the screen. "None of my business."

Hawk scowled, feeling torn. He didn't want to put

Laurie's reputation at risk, not for this, not when she'd been working so hard to be taken seriously, but he couldn't leave her in there wondering, either. He'd just pop in for a second to explain. They'd have another chance tomorrow. Or the next day.

His skin ached at the thought of delay. Never, he thought, walking as naturally as he could toward the bedroom, had he wanted a woman like this. And the weird thing was, it wasn't exactly physical, though that's how it manifested. If he could make love with his heart, he would do it. The thought was so corny he shook his head—he was always an idiot when he fell for a woman—but it was true. The wish to somehow complete the melding burned in him. He kept thinking of little things—that lemony smell; the way she'd changed her walk to fit that of a young girl with blond, curly hair; the scar on her arm.

He took a deep breath, steadying himself. He'd just take a minute, explain to her why they couldn't do anything tonight.

But when he knocked lightly and she called, "Come in," all those little things disappeared in his urgent, painful, furious need to touch her. She waited on the other side of the door in the dress and bare feet. Next to her on the floor was a pile of stockings, a silky something he thought might be a slip, and what was obviously a bra. She stood there, luminous and vivid, her chest rising and falling, her big eyes fastened on his face.

His heart slammed to a stop, then started again with a thud, and he thought he could feel extra blood flowing through him, heated to about five times its usual temperature. It made his hands shake as he locked the door and moved toward her, focused on her eyes.

With a toe, he kicked lightly at the pile of discarded undergarments, wanting to smile. But there was nothing in him but need, so he bent and put his arms around her, sighing as their bodies pressed close. For a minute it was almost too much, just the feeling of her next to him, and he buried his face in her neck. He swore softly, a release.

They just rocked together a little for the longest time, feeling, pressing close. The dress grew hot and wrinkled under his hands, and he moved his palms over her hips, up her back, closing his eyes so that all that existed was this, her shape against his palms.

"Kiss me, Hawk," she whispered, "before I die of wanting it."

He raised his head, trying dizzily to do the right thing. "They know we're doing this," he said. "Maybe we shouldn't. It'll ruin your reputation."

A blistering heat flashed in her eyes, and he realized that he'd known, somehow, that beneath that sweet, sunny exterior there would be a woman of deepest passion. She couldn't quite catch her breath as she stepped away, and regret ripped through him. He tried to be dignified, to straighten and take it like a man; it wasn't as if a delay would kill them.

She didn't smile as she shrugged. The tiny straps of the dress slipped down her arms. "I. Don't. Care." She said it in a husky voice, and slipped her arms out. "Do you want to do the rest, or shall I?"

He closed his eyes, thanking powers he hadn't really believed in for a long time. "Allow me," he said, and went forward, tugging slightly to free her breasts. The dress slid down to her waist and caught on her hips, and he thought he might die of pleasure right there, lifting his hands to her slim white shoulders, watching his dark fingers slide down the full slope of her firm, high breasts, watching the nipples tighten as his fingers crossed them. "You are so beautiful," he said, and bent his head to kiss her, first her mouth, deep and long, his hands cupping and caressing that heavy, soft weight, then her throat, then her mouth again. She cried out, her hands on his hips, pulling his shirt out of the waistband of his pants. She lifted her head. "Take it off."

"You do it. I don't want to take my hands off you." They swayed a little as the plane experienced slight turbulence, and he backed her against the wall for stability. "You want the bed?"

"No." She worked his buttons frantically, pushing the shirt off his shoulders, then sighing as she kissed his chest. He felt her settling slightly, as if an edge was taken off the urgency. He slid his arms around her, felt her own encircle him, her breasts and belly touching his chest. Then they kissed and touched, softly gliding and rocking against each other. He moved his hands on her back, and her skin was as smooth as he'd imagined. He skated them up and down, then farther down, over her bottom, still covered with the dress, and lower still, to her bare thighs. She made a soft, lost sound as he teased upward, and his sex burned as he found the swell of her buttocks; urgently, he sucked at her lips and then her neck, and slid down to his knees to kiss her breasts, his hands beneath her skirt.

Insane. Insane. He kissed her belly and then remembered the vision he'd had of her in that little gold skirt, and moved his hands around to the front of her thighs. Lifting his head with a smile, he looked up at her and pushed the skirt higher.

"Hawk," she said, breathing hard, a sheen of sweat over her skin, her eyes dark. "I don't think...I don't know...this is—"

He pushed the skirt up to her waist, then bent in close and put his tongue to the place he knew ached more than any other. Another little tremble of turbulence made him stop; she made a panting noise, and he could feel the trembling in her legs.

He stood and took her hand, then pushed her down on the bed. "I don't want either of us to get hurt," he said. And before he lay down with her, he unbuckled his pants and shed them, then the boxers, watching the heat in her eyes as she waited for him. He stood there, letting her look, as he looked. Her dark hair was spread across the white quilt, and the skirt was in a tangle around her waist. He reached up and pulled it off, leaving them both entirely naked, illuminated by soft little lamps, thirty-five thousand feet in the air.

"You have no idea," he said, his voice a harsh whisper, "how badly I want you right now."

She made a sound in her throat. "Oh, I think I do." She held out her hand. "Come here."

He fell over her, groaning softly at the feeling of naked skin touching his own, arms and legs, chests and bellies and thighs pressed together as they moved in a deep, hot, long kiss, her hands in his hair, his on her breasts and sides, hungry, so hungry. He was lost in her, totally lost, and it was the opposite of the feeling he'd had on the desert—that pieces of him were dissolving and blowing away. This felt like rain nourishing him, damp and warm and sweet—their lips and tongues sinuous and sliding, her breasts supple and soft, her body quivering and as hungry as his own.

And he wanted to linger, to make it last, but when she shifted, opening to him, he lifted his head, planning somehow to say something. Instead he was caught by the deep yearning in her eyes, and he could only position himself and slide home. He watched her, and saw her head fall backward as she arched into him, reached for his shoulders, pulled him down and in, and Hawk let go, fell into the magic, the depth and power of the light that rushed through him.

He let himself go, loving her and not minding it, a soft litany in his mind. *Why not something good? Why not?*

Laurie cradled Hawk's head against her shoulder, her hand clasped gently over the back of his neck, his breath on her throat. She could feel the remnants of their spent energy pulsing through her body. He kissed her lightly, her neck and jaw, as he lifted his head.

There was no need for words as they looked at each other, and Laurie wasn't sure she could find language, anyway. His long black hair fell around his dark, beautiful face as he looked at her, straight in the eye, with such openness it made her ache all over again. He bent and brushed her lips with his own, moving his hips subtly, a movement she mimicked, the lingering heat of satisfaction met and returned. His eyelashes, inky and thick, seemed the most beautiful thing she'd ever seen. She touched his hair, twined strands of it around her fingers, admiring the color and weight of it.

In time, they sighed and parted, scrambling together beneath the covers for warmth. Laurie laughed softly as she snuggled into the place he made for her on his shoulder. "I bet most people don't make it into the mile-high club with so much comfort."

His laughter rumbled through his chest, the warmest sound she'd ever heard. "I'm pretty sure not." His hands moved on her softly, and he shifted to look at her. "I need to see you," he said quietly, lying on his side so they faced each other. "Look at you." He touched her forehead with the tips of his fingers, tracing her hairline and temple, her ear and jaw and lips, following each movement with his gaze. His expression was serious and enchanted at once, and Laurie had never felt so treasured or beautiful in her life. It made her chest hurt.

Especially because looking at him seemed so right, as if she'd known his face before, somewhere. That particular nose, high-bridged and arrogant; those green-glass eyes; the hollow below his cheekbone that caught the light in a long oval... She had known these hands in another life, and the sheen of his walnut-colored skin.

"When I first met you," she said, putting her hand on his jaw, "I thought you were dangerous. Like a tiger. I thought you would be rough as a lover."

A glimmer of amusement crinkled his eyes. "Sweet savage love, huh?"

She laughed. "No. I mean, yeah, but not because you're Indian. You just seemed so tightly coiled."

"I was." He cupped his palm over the curve of her shoulder, smoothed his hand down her arm. "Everything was so dark all the time. You're like sunlight, Laurie. That's corny, I know it is, but that night in the dressing room, that's what you felt like—like sunlight. Bright yellow."

His words pierced her. "Really?"

"Don't let it go to your head or anything," he said with a cynical little smile.

"I'll try."

He moved the covers down to her waist, and with the same attention he'd given her hair and face and shoulder, he touched her chest, then her breasts, one finger circling one nipple, then the other. Gently, he cupped the flesh in his hand and murmured, "So beautiful," then raised himself on one elbow to bend over her and lift that breast to his mouth. He was slow about it, moving his head back and forth, just those soft lips, then he sighed and opened his mouth, gliding that tongue over the same place. A thousand new points of desire ignited in Laurie's body and she made a small noise of pleasure.

He smiled up at her, a very wicked smile, then bent his head again. And tortured her, tasting her, pressing his mouth and tongue all over her torso, then against the crook of her inner elbow, then someplace unexpected like her chin. Laurie quivered beneath the sweet heat of it, so different from what she'd imagined, this slow, exquisite style. He was braced on one elbow, but used the other hand to tease her body, her sides and legs, drawing light patterns over her belly, along the intensely sensitive flesh of her inner thighs, then higher, and away again.

Laurie caught his hand. "Wait!"

"What?"

She pushed at his shoulder and sat up next to him, tugging the covers from his long, beautiful body. She smiled, a little shakily, as she touched him back. Caressed him the way he'd stroked her, all over, raining kisses on him, circling his sex with her hand, admiring it. "Very nice," she whispered.

"It's all yours, honey."

So they made love again, and Laurie liked it that the room was bright enough so she could see his face as he looked at her, so she could look at him, so it wasn't some secret act done in the dark, but unabashed and clear and somehow honest. She loved it when he grew too aroused to go slowly anymore, and urgently pulled her face to his, kissing her as they climaxed, in a crescendo again, first him, then her, and fell in a sweaty tangle of exhausted limbs and panting breath. Curled together afterward, they did not speak at all, only drifted into a sated, contented sleep.

An hour or so later, Hawk realized he was starving. "Are you hungry?"

"Famished," she said, tossing hair out of her face. "But all the food is on the other side of the plane."

"Maybe they've fallen asleep."

"It's a mission worth undertaking," she said. "Agent Stone, shall I, or do you wish to mount the effort?"

"You don't move. I want you naked forever."

"I don't think that's possible." She shifted languorously. "But you can probably get another hour or two."

He got up and put on his pants and shirt, even tucking it in.

"Better use a comb," Laurie said, chuckling.

He was already taking one out of his back pocket. "Way ahead of you." He finished and returned it to his pocket. "Be back in a flash."

He opened the door quietly and saw that both agents were stretched out fast asleep, the television screen showing the blank darkness of a finished movie. Hawk crept past them quietly, praying no turbulence would upset his balance, and made it safely to the galley. He took a bottle of red wine out of the rack, then started collecting tidbits that looked good—a pair of apples, half a loaf of French bread, some tiny cheeses wrapped in wax, chocolate. He grinned, thinking it looked like hiking supplies. A vigorous sport, sex.

The stuff was too incriminating so he scoured around, looking for something to carry it in. In a drawer, he found a cloth bag and settled it all in there gently, then headed back.

Alex, the blond agent, blinked at him sleepily. "What time is it?"

"About two, I think. Got another hour or so."

He nodded, yawning. "Well, have fun. One of us might as well."

Hawk froze. With narrowed eyes, he bent close. "This is none of your business," he said in his most threatening voice. "Are we clear?"

"Yes, sir. Sorry."

"Not a word, man. I mean it."

He lifted a hand. "I swear."

Hawk left him, but a little of the sheen was off his mood when he went back into the room. Laurie sat on the bed, covers pulled up over her breasts, her back against the wall. Her hair was tousled, her eyes sultry from their evening, but she picked up on his mood immediately. "Are they awake?"

"One of them." Hawk put the bag on the bed and started unloading it. "Oh, hell, I forgot glasses."

"We can drink from the bottle," she said, smiling. "It'll be a picnic."

"You're just a wild woman beneath that good-girl exterior, aren't you?"

Soft color rose in her cheeks. "Not usually."

And suddenly, nothing else mattered but this, Laurie and him in this pocket of time they'd stolen—not yesterday, not tomorrow. Only now. He sat down and kissed her. "I'm glad it's just for me."

"Don't let it go to your head," she said, raising her eyebrows. "Get your clothes off and give me food now."

He chuckled. "Aye-aye, Captain."

She opened the wine and took a fingernail to the wax on the cheese as he undressed and climbed in next to her. Beneath them the engines hummed, and he thought of the world, so far away. "I gotta tell ya, there are things about being rich I wouldn't mind."

"Me, too. The clothes, mainly."

"Really? At the heart of it, you don't really seem like the type to care."

"Oh, you would be wrong." She freed the baby cheese and bit into it. "All I did as a young teenager was pour over beauty magazines. I love clothes, and I never really got to have what I wanted, you know? My mother didn't approve of frivolities in clothes. I could have one or two good dresses for church, but they had to wash and dry easily, and of course they couldn't be sexy." She examined the cheese. "But even if I'd had permission, there wouldn't have been anywhere to buy the clothes I wanted, or anywhere to wear them, come to that."

Hawk lifted the wine and took a long swallow. "I guess I can understand that. There was a leather jacket at a store in Flagstaff that I burned for at about age sixteen. I figured if I wore it, no girl in town could say no to me.''

"As if they did, anyway."

"Trust me, they said it a lot." He handed her the bottle and picked up an apple, remembering. "I was skinny as hell and way too earnest."

"I would have been madly in love with you, then."

"Yeah?"

"Yes. My brothers and all their friends were so obnoxiously sure they were God's gift to women that I just hated them. I got a really close view of the disgusting habits of boys early on."

"Mmm." The apple was sweet and crisp. One of the ten best things he'd ever tasted. "But I bet you wouldn't have said yes."

"Probably not. I was a very good girl in those days."

"Still are."

"And you're still earnest."

That stung, somewhere deep. He looked at her. "Only with you." A creeping sense of fear invaded him suddenly. "What are we doing, Laurie?"

Her eyes were as guileless as dawn as she met his gaze. "I think we're falling in love, that's all."

"In love for now, or is it all going to be different when we get back to real life?"

"I don't know. But it's really nice right now, isn't it? Maybe we ought to just enjoy it."

"But what if one of us gets hurt?"

She lifted one bare, beautiful shoulder. "Speaking for myself, it was worth it."

He kissed her urgently. "I want to be like you when I grow up," he growled. "Just like you."

Chapter 13

The next day passed in a blur for Laurie. She was as languorous as a cat once they got to the hotel, and tried hard to act normally—whatever that looked like. She and Hawk were attended by the new agents, and in the end, it seemed easier to just retreat to her own bedroom and sleep. She didn't want to think too much just yet, and in spite of her reassurances to Hawk about the future being worth what happened now, she was fairly sure it wasn't going to end in some happily ever after scenario.

And she didn't want to think about that.

The final public appearance of the princess was at a fund-raiser for children with disabilities. Laurie had slept most of the day, making up for the long, lovely night with Hawk on the plane. As she prepared for the evening, washing her hair, putting on stockings and makeup, choosing undergarments from the wonderful selection available, little memories pricked her now and again, rich, hot thorns of emotion—the way he looked dozing, all the pressure and defenses dropping away. His hand, loose and relaxed on the cover over her tummy, the fingers long and brown and beautiful. The length of his beautiful back, muscled and supple. She wondered if there was any chance they'd have some time alone tonight.

The evening itself was, in a word, boring. Laurie had grown comfortable with her role as Julia, and hardly had to think about it anymore. She made small talk with matrons, and with men who wanted to press a bit too close to her. Hawk stayed right beside her, his hand sometimes lingering just a little longer than necessary as he escorted her from place to place. She felt his tenseness at the function, his wary alertness, but she herself was perfectly relaxed. There was absolutely no sense of danger in this place.

At one point, they found themselves alone in a pocket of space near a wall. Laurie sipped a glass of wine, keeping her gaze focused on the people around them. "Do you suppose we might get rid of our watchdogs anytime soon?" she asked.

"Doesn't look like it, does it?"

Laurie sighed. "Not really." She gave him a quick glance. "Maybe we'll get to take off tonight again. I could slip them a mickey. It's not a very long flight to Aspen, but it would be an hour or two."

Discreetly, he touched her back. "The weather isn't promising for that scenario."

And that much was true. Thunderstorms had been threatening all afternoon, boiling up across the country. "Well, use your imagination, huh?"

Her back was to the wall and he slid his hand down

to her fanny. "I can do that," he said, his voice going liquid. "Right now."

Laurie fought the ripple of anticipation that rolled over her at that husky note, and managed to keep her face perfectly calm. "I don't know if that's a great idea." She was wearing the red dress, after all. It showed too much as it was.

But Hawk chose to ignore her. "I'm imagining you do not have on any panties," he said quietly in her ear. "I'm imagining us standing before a mirror, and me taking down the straps of that dress to reveal your beautiful, beautiful breasts, and I'm watching you in the mirror as you see my hands on you."

Her heart pattered. "I think you need to stop now."

His hand lightly moved on her bottom, brushed her thighs, and Laurie felt every nerve in her body go on instant alert. "I'm imagining that I'm pulling up this skirt, just a little at a time, and your breath is coming faster and faster, and then I free myself and take you right there, both of us looking in the mirror."

She said, "Make it so, Captain," and turned around to give him a look before she put the wine down. "I'll be in the ladies' room."

He caught her arm. "Not here!"

"Oh, of course not!" She smiled, very faintly. "I'm going to take off my panties."

A band of heat burned on his cheekbones. "I was only teasing you."

"That's all I'm going to do."

He closed his eyes. "I'll die."

She grinned. "I don't think so."

But he nearly did. She returned from the powder room with a high flush on her cheeks, and Hawk was forced to attend her for nearly two hours, imagining nothing beneath the long red skirt but her bare bottom.

And he didn't know if it was his imagination torturing him, but it seemed every man in the room felt the same way. Over and over, she ended up in the middle of a circle of doting men, most of them older political types. They hung on her every word, admiring the fine milky skin, the swell of breasts above the bodice, the tiniest hint of nipples beneath her armoring bra.

Hawk had never had such an agonizing, unending erection in his life, and kept his coat firmly buttoned even when the room grew hot.

The terrible thing was, he knew there was no chance for them to be alone. Mutt and Jeff, aka Alex and Dave, waited for them in the limo, full of cheery bits about a baseball game on the radio. They rode up with them in the hotel elevator, oblivious to the tension. Hawk stood next to Laurie at the back, aching to put his hands on her, and she leaned comfortably against the wall, her pinching shoes in her hand. He tried not to look at her bare toes, the nails painted red.

He especially tried not to notice when Laurie dropped her shoes by the door and went to the large mirror on the wall above a table, to take the pins out of her hair. She met his eyes in the mirror, and he said, "Guys, don't you want to get out and see the sights? Take the limo, go to a club. We don't leave until ten in the morning."

"Let me clear it with headquarters," Dave said. "That'd be good."

Alex smirked, or so it seemed to Hawk, but he didn't care.

The call was made, approval was given and Hawk closed the door behind them with relief. He bolted it and turned toward Laurie, who looked like a movie star in the red dress, her hair loose in waves around her shoulders.

"You were saying?" she said, leaning against the table.

He tossed off his jacket and crossed the room in three steps, his blood roaring. With urgent hands, he took her shoulders and turned her to face the mirror, then roughly pulled the straps of her dress down revealing the black strapless bra that contained her breasts. He bent and bit her neck as he found the clasp for the bra, biting and sucking gently, up and down, as her breasts were freed. He felt nearly violent in his need, and from the shine in her eyes and the tenseness of her breath, he knew it was as electrifying for her.

Staring at her in the mirror, he took her breasts in his hands and rolled the nipples between his fingers. Her nostrils flared, and she reached behind herself and touched him, working his buckle as he rubbed his hands over her, down, over the red silk pooled around her waist, boldly touching the triangle shape between her legs through the dress, groaning as she freed him, her fingers fluttering over his sex. And she wasn't shy about it.

With a roar, he pulled up the skirt and found she had indeed shed the panties. He swallowed, amazed at how unbelievably sexy her long legs looked, how great the entire view of bare rear and red skirt was. He took her hips and thrust hard, and she braced herself against the table, crying out in pleasure, and he held her there for a second, looking at them in the mirror, bending together. "You are so outrageously sexy," he rasped, and there was no more talk.

Laurie could not believe how wild it was, how exciting, to be so wicked. She loved the way she looked, how intense Hawk's eyes were as he took her. She loved the erotic movements of his hands on her, the sexy rush at seeing their reflections. She thrilled a little to the roughness.

But it only seemed to fuel some furiously powerful imagination in both of them. They teased and taunted and played. It wasn't enough, ever. She took him in the shower, with water pouring over them, and on her bed, and on the chair.

Finally somewhat sated—and a little shaky—they took big glasses of milk and grapes into his bedroom and curled up in matching hotel robes on his bed, looking out at the city through the long windows. Laurie rested her back against his chest, feeling a little shy as she thought about the craziness. "Are we terribly wicked, Hawk?"

His arm tightened around her. "Probably. Gonna burn in hell for this, no doubt." She heard the laughter in his tone. "It'll be worth it, though, eh?"

"You're not shocked or anything, are you?"

"What do you mean?"

She shrugged a little, touching his arm for reassurance. "I mean, that was pretty bad, walking around on the job without my underwear." She flushed, just thinking about it. "I honestly don't know what came over me. I've never done anything like that in my life!"

"You think I might be shocked at you, you mean?"

"Well..."

He pulled her sideways into the crook of his arm, and she thought, suddenly, that she really loved how he did that. It made her feel safe and close to him. "I have never had such great sex in my life, Laurie. I mean it." He opened his palm on her face. "I love it that you're so uninhibited, and that you—" he looked sober suddenly "—feel free enough with me to let that side of you show."

She just looked up at him for a long moment. "It really was fun."

He grinned, showing his white teeth. "Oh, yeah."

Laurie kissed him quickly and slipped out of his grasp, leaning on one elbow. "So, James, tell me how you got the nickname Hawk. I have to tell you it's almost corny."

"Yeah, I know. But my mom called me that, and I like it for that reason. I found a baby hawk when I was little and took it to her. She helped me nurse it back to health and then we let it go." His eyes were far away, and he touched her hand without seeming to know it. "She said that she would call me Hawk so that I'd always remember to be strong and wise like that, and gentle like the boy who found it."

"Oh, that's a wonderful story! What was she like, your mom?"

"Very beautiful and gentle. I look a lot like her, except my eyes."

She grinned. "So you're very beautiful?"

"You betcha. What I really remember is her hair. She had very, very long hair, and she braided it every morning."

"I don't know how you stood losing her at, what? Eight or nine, didn't you say?"

"It was hard," he said, his voice gravelly all of a sudden. "I just didn't see how you could be in that much pain and still live."

A sudden insight struck her. "That's what hurts you about that boy, isn't it?"

"Boy?"

"Yeah, the one who survived the shooting. He lost his mother, like you did."

Hawk looked at her in a kind of horror. "I don't want to think about that right now. I can't, okay?"

"Okay," she said easily. "I'm sorry."

"No, don't be." He blew out a breath. "Sooner or later, I'm gonna have to deal with it. Just not to-night."

"Fair enough." She jumped up. "Do you mind if I paint my fingernails? I have some chips I want to fix."

"No. I actually think it's kind of sexy."

"Be right back, then." She closed her bedroom door on the way, so the agents would think she was in there instead of with Hawk. How she'd get from one room to the other with the two of them camped in the sitting room was another worry for another time.

Settling on the bed, cross-legged, she shook the bottle. "So, let's play twenty questions, okay?"

"Twenty questions? Like, truth-or-dare stuff?" He wiggled his eyebrows.

"Well, not necessarily. Just little things. I'll go first—do you like cats or dogs better?"

"Hmm." He stuck out his lower lip. "I like 'em

both. I already know you like cats and you miss having one.''

"Hey, you're good." She set the bottle of polish on the nightstand. "Now you ask me one."

He thought for a minute. "Who did you lose your virginity to?"

Laurie was startled and looked up from her painting. "That's fairly deep."

"I want to know about you. If you don't want to say, it's all right."

"No, I guess I don't mind." Carefully, she stroked red lacquer on her left forefinger. "It was at college. Donald Hazel. We dated for most of my freshman year."

"Where did you go?"

"To his dorm room." She grinned. "It wasn't very good, I have to admit." She finished the left hand and raised her head. "My turn." And suddenly, it was hard to think of which thing to ask, what secret he might reveal in the midst of mundanities. She felt a vast and needy wish to know all there was to know about him. "What's your favorite movie?"

"Don't see many movies. Let's see…Steven Segal is pretty cool."

She rolled her eyes. "Don't tell me you're an action adventure guy."

"I'm a cop. My dad's a mercenary, or at least I think he is." He smiled. "My turn."

Laurie grinned. "Sure, go ahead."

He licked his bottom lip, eyes narrowing. "What's the saddest thing you remember?"

She looked at him, feeling an odd tension in him, a sense that she needed to answer this question just right. What was hanging in the balance here? Did he want to know the bad things she'd survived, or that she'd known grief? "I'm not sure what you're asking," she said at last. "I haven't had the kind of tragedies in my life that you have."

"There had to be sad things, Laurie."

"Well, of course there were. When we had to bury our sixteen-year-old dog, I cried for two days. When my brother and his wife got divorced, it was terrible for everybody. The tornado was awful. I was very sad when my grandfather died." She paused. "But nothing like you've known, Hawk. Really."

She couldn't tell, looking at him, if it made him feel better or worse, and suddenly, from the other room, came voices. The agents were back. She widened her eyes and put a careful finger—her nails were still wet—to her lips.

A sultry, wicked expression crossed his mouth, and he said, barely audible, "You can't touch anything, can you?"

She shook her head.

"And we have to be really quiet, right?"

She nodded. Judging from the racket on the other side of the door, the boys had been partying a bit. One kicked something and swore. She chuckled.

Hawk moved slowly toward her, reaching for the tie around her waist. "I can't believe I want you again," he said, pulling open the robe, "but this is just too good." He pushed her backward and opened his mouth on her breast, and unbelievably, Laurie felt a response ripple through her instantly. "Hawk—"

"Shh. Don't move. Don't say a word."

And it was sweet and hot at once, the feeling of his lips closing over her breast, the sense of him easing, so slowly, into her, gentle and careful to make up for the athleticism of the evening. When they were joined once again, he raised his head and kissed her deeply, and she tasted again that lost need, that vast hunger, and she knew she had given him only temporary respite from his demons.

She put her arms around his neck and clasped him tightly to her, kissing him back with all the feeling she could muster, wishing it could be more.

So much more.

Chapter 14

Hawk awakened to warm sunlight streaming in his hotel windows, falling in puddles over his arms and chest and cheek. It pooled on the top of Laurie's back beneath her hair, caressing that tender spot between her shoulder blades. She was turned away from him, her face buried in the pillow, her hair in a wild spray over her face and pillow. He shifted to his side to look at her.

Even in this bright, unrelenting light, her skin was so flawless it amazed him. Her hair gleamed with red highlights. Only the tip of her nose was visible beneath it.

He didn't touch her, but simply looked at her, aware of a vast feeling of tenderness and contentment, something so much larger than himself that it seemed to fill the room.

From where he lay, he could see the city spreading away to the horizon, and he remembered, suddenly, standing at the window in the hotel in D.C., feeling lost and dried up and dull. It seemed a long time ago. How could so much have changed in him so fast? How could he trust such a transformation?

And in a way, wasn't it a betrayal of John to let him go?

A soft pop of recognition sounded in his head at that. Was that what was at the heart of all this? Did Hawk believe that he gave John honor by holding on to his grief? That by letting go, he would be letting go of his friend's life?

Hawk shifted a little, and Laurie stirred the smallest bit, making a quiet sound as she moved. She was close to waking up, but not quite there. He smiled fondly, admiring her mouth. What a woman she was! Both innocent and powerful. Did the power come from innocence? Was it only in tragedy that people lost confidence in the world? If that was so, he would do whatever was necessary to protect her forever from discovering what tragedy could do to a person. Her joy in living was palpable, and infectious and the world needed it.

How could he let her face the terrorists? His stomach lurched.

His father's face suddenly appeared on his mental screen, unrelated to the jumble of thoughts in Hawk's mind. Or *was* it unrelated?

Shifting quietly, he lay on his back and stared at the ceiling. His father. Who had survived Vietnam and the death of his beloved Lorena, and who had not only faced death and trauma, but actively sought out situations where they might occur.

Situations in which he might *prevent* them.

Hawk cleared his throat. Maybe that was the real

trick here. Realize what could be gained instead of what had been lost. Was it really that simple? Change focus and change his life? He wanted it to be true. So much.

"Uh-oh," Laurie said next to him. "That's a very serious expression. Brooding so early?"

He made a place for her on his chest, sliding an arm around her shoulder. "Not exactly. I'm just wondering how much of this we can trust."

She rubbed his chest softly. "Maybe you shouldn't worry about it right now, Hawk."

He was silent for a long moment. "I don't think I can let the terrorists take you, Laurie."

"You might not have a choice."

"What if I asked you to give this up now?" He looked at her. "Just let it go."

Her blue eyes were steady and unafraid, unblinking. "You know the answer to that question."

"But—" He stopped himself, only thinking the rest of it: *but what if I lose you?*

"You have to trust me, Hawk." She lifted on one elbow to look at him earnestly. "You have to trust that I can do my job."

"I don't distrust you," he said. "What if they hurt you? What if they rape you?"

She didn't smile. "The possibility has crossed my mind, too, Hawk. But this is why we're doing it. We're in law enforcement so that we can help protect people—innocent people—who don't have the tools that we do." She paused. "We all know that we take a risk when we say we'll do the job."

Involuntarily, his eye twitched, and a fragment of memory sizzled into his mind—blood and noise and gunshots. "Maybe the risk in this situation is too high."

She set her jaw. "No, Hawk, it isn't." She pulled away, turning her back to him as she shoved her arms into the sleeves of a robe. Only when it was secured and she was safely covered did she turn to face him. "Don't do this."

He looked away. "All I'm asking is that you think about what it might be like."

"To do what?" she challenged. "To get gang raped, to get killed, to get beaten? Do you honestly think I haven't thought about it? I have, and I'm willing to take the risk. If they don't kill me, I'd survive the rest. It's my job to do that.

"It's my job to keep Julia Sebastiani safe," she said, and there was fury and frustration in her tone. "She is beloved—you've seen that. It would be awful if something happened to her, and I'm not going to let it."

"Laurie—"

"Save it," she said, and stormed out.

Hawk fell back on the bed, swearing under his breath. "That went well," he said aloud to the ceiling.

The trip to Aspen was uneventful. The two agents traveled with Hawk and Laurie, and the four of them played poker to pass the time. The flight was bumpy; according to the pilot, it was thanks to unstable air caused by thunderstorms boiling over most of the south.

But it didn't cause any particular discomfort, and when they landed in Aspen, it was a sparkling, almost achingly beautiful day. "Oh, my gosh!" Laurie exclaimed as she stepped onto the tarmac. "This is amazing!"

"Ever been to Colorado before?" Alex asked her.

"No," she said in awe, turning in a slow circle to take it all in. The sky was such a deep, rich blue it looked unnatural, as if someone had stretched blue rubber over the roof of the world. Rising into that depth of color were craggy mountaintops covered with furry green. "I always thought mountains were blue."

Hawk took her arm. Laurie, still furious with him, pulled free and glared at him. He gave her a look. "The princess would not be astonished, honey. She's been here a lot."

"Oh, sorry." She composed herself. "I'll gawk when we get to the cabin."

"Cabin," Alex echoed. "What d'you want to bet it's five-thousand square feet of luxury?"

"No bet from me," Laurie said with a laugh.

A car and driver waited for them—no limo this time, but a silver Mercedes, the princess's own car. A second car was parked behind it, a standard invisible FBI sedan, and the driver came forward to tell Alex and Dave they were going to be housed in town. The princess, it appeared, did not like much staff when she was not making appearances. There would be agents posted at the perimeter of the property, disguised as groundsmen, and the usual cook had been replaced with security, but that was it.

Once in the car, Hawk and Laurie were briefed by the driver, who relayed the plan to draw out the kidnappers. They were to behave in a holiday fashion, go to dinner and see the sights, just relax, which was what the princess usually did here. The FBI hoped the kidnappers would strike again within the week. Because of the self-contained world high in the mountains, FBI agents would have a better chance of capturing the ringleaders, get the information they needed to bust the group for good.

"Sounds reasonable," Laurie said.

Hawk looked out the window, and she knew he was thinking she couldn't handle the job. But he would not undermine her confidence like this. She wouldn't allow it.

As they drove through the idyllic setting, brilliant in the high-altitude sunlight, Laurie realized that Julia's brother's plane had gone down around here somewhere. "Is there any word of Prince Lucas?" she asked.

"None," the driver said. "It's not looking good."

"How tragic."

"It is, indeed."

The three of them fell silent, until they arrived at the "cabin." Laurie stepped out of the car and laughed in pleasure. Behind her, Hawk whistled, low and long. The house, built of attractively weathered logs, was situated in a high glade surrounded by a thick forest of dark pines mixed with the glittery pale aspens that had given the town its name. Generous balconies overlooked a vista of mountains and valleys rolling away into the distance beneath that bright sky.

Behind her, Hawk said, "Wow."

"Yeah." Laurie allowed herself a wink. "Tough being a princess."

He smiled reluctantly.

Weary of playing to an audience twenty-four hours a day, Laurie ducked out of her duties and found a bathing suit to lounge in next to a courtyard pool inlaid with mosaic tiles. It was a brilliantly sunny day, very quiet, and ignoring Hawk altogether, she asked for sandwiches and soda water with lime to be served outside. She turned on the radio to an oldies station, and after a good hard swim, draped herself over a lawn chair to doze in the sun.

After a little while, Hawk came out. "Mind if I join you?"

"Are you going to be my partner or my older brother?"

He raised his brows with a faint smile. "I was kinda hoping for something else entirely."

Laurie smiled. "Now that's more like it."

He dropped down beside her, shedding shoes and shirt to reveal the length of his dark torso, his sexy, strong legs. "I'd kiss you, but they'd see." His green eyes were brilliant in the bright sun, making him look like a statue set with emerald eyes. Her heart flipped a little, and she brushed his shin with the tips of her fingers. "I can wait."

She was smart enough to realize the problem had not entirely been solved, but she was also content to let it be this afternoon. Just for a few hours, she would accept the status quo. "Let's just take it easy this afternoon, huh?"

"Good idea." He stood. "I'm going to swim for a while."

He dived in like an arrow, slicing into the blue, and Laurie decided that there was absolutely nothing he could do to look bad. The water sluiced through his dark hair and over his richly colored skin, making him seem like a creature of the deep, a seal, maybe. When he emerged after a while to bake in the sun next to her in a lounge chair, she simply gave herself up to admiring how beautiful he was.

But the sun made her sleepy and she drifted a little, her thoughts turning to Julia, who had lain in this very chair, likely protecting her skin with sunblock, a hat and a cover-up, just as Laurie had to. This was Julia's home, with its beautiful paintings and graceful touches.

And somewhere out there, in those mountains, was the secret to her brother's disappearance. It made Laurie sad to think it might be his body they would find.

"Have you ever noticed that the princess seems kind of sad?" she said in a low voice.

"Mmm. I don't know."

Laurie didn't realize she'd been thinking about it, but suddenly several bits came together. "There are a lot of pictures from when she's younger, looking really happy and energetic and full of life. When she got married, that changed." Laurie opened her eyes to look at Hawk. "What do you think happened with those two?"

"I have no idea."

Classic man answer. "Poor thing. Now she's pregnant by the son of her father's enemy, and her brother is probably dead, and even her lover has disappeared. I feel sorry for her."

"Yeah, so do I, in a way. Poor little rich princess."

Laurie frowned. "That's mean."

"Yeah," he agreed, opening his eyes halfway. The sharp sunlight turned them a vivid green, as if some magical animal was lurking beneath those heavy lids. "I know money doesn't make everything perfect, but sometimes it's hard to remember that."

"It's like Romeo and Juliet or something."

"Or Rashid and Julia." He chuckled.

Laurie smiled, closing her eyes once more. The radio played nearby and Laurie hummed along with a sweet ballad, drifting on her thoughts, wondering vaguely if she'd ever get to meet the princess. And wondering, too, what Julia had thought of the public portrayals Laurie had delivered. Was the princess embarrassed or pleased? Or was she so sad that she simply didn't care?

At the end of a song, the news came on, and Laurie got up to go change the station. As she reached the set, however, the headliner story came on and her hand froze in midair. "One of the worst tornadoes in recent memory struck just an hour ago in Little Bend, Oklahoma. Details are pouring in, and we go now to our correspondent on the scene."

"Oh, damn," she said. "I have to go see this."

"What?" Hawk asked, lifting his head and blinking in a way that spoke volumes about his drowsiness.

"Tornado in Oklahoma. I'm going in to the TV."

"I thought you weren't supposed to take in bad news?" he called, but she just waved a hand and kept going, wrapping a gauzy robe around her as she padded inside. There was a television in a den off the main hallway, and she turned it on with the remote control, standing in the middle of the room as she ran through channels rapidly, settling finally on CNN. News crews were already on the scene.

A chill went through her, and she crossed her arms protectively. It seemed impossible that the day could be so sunny and perfect here, when only a state or two distant, it looked like this. Rain fell on the scene of the disaster, and the reporter wore a yellow rain hat. In the background were sticks and litter, a dented car. "We're live from Little Bend, Oklahoma, where just an hour ago, a massive tornado roared through the town. You can see behind me to the scene of destruction where homes, businesses and pretty much everything else has been flattened."

Laurie felt Hawk come in behind her, but her attention was riveted to the screen, where aerial photos were showing the path of the tornado. Gooseflesh rose on her arms. It never ceased to astonish her the way storms could move across a stretch of land with such preciseness, demolishing everything in their path, and leaving everything on either side untouched. So strange. Storms were almost alive, she sometimes thought. Some manifestation of intelligent evil afoot in the world.

"It was a bad one," she said, covering her mouth with her fingers as the cameras focused on people wandering the streets, picking through the rubble. Sirens roared and a little girl cried. Cars were overturned, the camera focused on a truck that had been deposited in a tree and fallen down, breaking branches all the way to the ground. There was hardly anything left standing; the twister had left a path of splinters. Laurie swallowed. "A really bad one."

Her usual tears welled up, and in spite of Hawk's presence, she let them fall. It was a coping mechanism, someone had told her, a method of managing her terrible memories. She nearly always cried when there was a bad storm shown on the news, and she always sent money. It was something she could do to combat the devastation.

Hawk touched her shoulder, obviously concerned, but not making judgments, and she loved him for that. "Pretty bad," he said.

She looked at him wordlessly, then back at the screen. More demolished buildings, more places where something had been and now wasn't. Rubble and mess everywhere. The reporter's voice-over said, "Seventeen people are confirmed dead, and many dozens more are still missing in the aftermath of what scientists are saying was the worst tornado in this country since the 1987 destruction of Broken Wheel, Nebraska."

Laurie grabbed Hawk's arm. "That's my hometown! Look!" The screen flashed to a scene of what had once been the downtown area, as utterly destroyed as if a bomb had gone off. Glass and litter and rubble marked the streets, and one lone wall, untouched, the window still in it, stood straight up with no visible support. Once, Laurie knew, it had been the diner. The wall had fallen down the next day.

"That's your town?" Hawk said.

"Yep." Laurie crossed her arms, feeling a chill in spite of the sunny day.

"Is it your tornado?"

She nodded. "Yes."

"Damn," he said quietly.

More photos flashed, file footage someone had dug up very quickly. The reporter gave the statistics on the terrible tornado that had struck that summer: 23 people dead, 69 wounded.

One of the latter had been Laurie.

She touched the scar on her arm, remembering, her mind filled up with recalled details as it sometimes did. The news flashed back to Oklahoma and the tornado just past, but Laurie was twelve, back in Broken Wheel, scrambling to her feet after the tornado finally moved on.

"I was in the loft," she said. "And I heard it just before it struck—an unbelievable roar, like the worst monster you can imagine, like the beasts of hell. It roared right into the barn and sucked me up, and I was so scared I wet my pants. I remember being inside of it, seeing all this darkness, hearing the roar of it.

"And then it was over. I was on the ground and my arm hurt so bad that I knew it was broken. I'd cut my head, right above the eyebrow, so of course it was bleeding as if I was dying." She smiled up at Hawk and discovered he was listening intently, his eyes soft and compassionate.

She swallowed. "At first, I thought it was because of the blood that I couldn't see anything." Unconsciously, she took the position she had then, right arm cradling the left. "I turned around in a circle, and there was nothing. I turned and turned and turned, and it didn't matter where I looked—there was nothing left. No house. No barn. No cars or equipment or tractors or clothesline. The leaves were stripped off the tree by the old back door, but there wasn't a door." She paused for a moment, taking a breath. "I felt like the last human in the world."

"This tornado that broke your arm took the house and barn?"

"Yep."

"And you lived through it."

She smiled. "Obviously. So did my whole family. Even the dogs and most of the cats. A couple of them disappeared, you know. We never saw them again. And of course we lost the horses and cattle." She paused, aching even now, so many years later, for the horse she'd loved. They'd found him, finally, in a gully twenty miles away. "But everything else made it."

"Where was your family? Why didn't they come get you?"

"They went to the storm cellar. They'd looked for me, but I was hiding from my brothers."

"Did the whole town get hit that hard?"

Laurie nodded, looking up again at the television screen. "Pretty much. It bankrupted my father, and quite a few other people." She pointed at a young family staring at the remains of a house. "They're the ones I feel sorry for—everything all demolished, just like that. Blink of an eye." She snapped her fingers. "Gone."

"So what did you do? Where did you go? Afterward, I mean."

"We didn't go anywhere," she said. "People brought in trailers and lived in campers and tents—whatever. The Red Cross helped a lot, and by the time it got cold, most of us had some kind of shelter. My parents got most of the downstairs rebuilt by winter. We slept on cots."

He rubbed her arms wordlessly, and Laurie realized she was trembling a bit, remembering it all. She gazed up at him steadily. "Now you see why I hate tornadoes."

He nodded, his mouth tight. After a minute, he let go of a breath. "Why don't we go into town, get some supper?" he suggested.

Laurie lifted her head. Work as distraction... She smiled. "You're learning, aren't you?"

"Learning what?" He seemed genuinely bewildered.

"Never mind. Let's go to town, bodyguard. Let me go put on my princess hat."

Happily, Julia did own casual clothes for her stays in Aspen, and Laurie was relieved to choose a pair of khaki slacks and low-heeled shoes with a crisp, but casual blouse she tucked in. She thought about leaving her hair down, but put it in a French braid at the last minute. It helped her remember to stay in character.

The driver had arranged a reservation at a small Italian bistro the princess went to everytime she was in Aspen, and drove them into town, a charming village set at the foot of a huge mountain Laurie assumed was the ski slope that made the place so famous. Hawk, playing the solicitous bodyguard, gave her a wink as they stepped out of the car. Quietly, he said, "Amazingly beautiful."

"I agree."

The owner of the restaurant greeted her cheerily and fussed over her, but the ubiquitous bowing and scraping that had marked so many of their encounters was missing, and Laurie realized there had been no paparazzi outside, either. The reason became plain once they sat down and looked around. A senator sat in shorts and shirtsleeves near the window, eating supper with a young teen who was obviously his son. A pair of movie stars were nestled near a potted palm, obviously expecting not to be stared at. When the waiter scurried off to bring the princess's bottled water, Laurie leaned over the table with a wicked grin. "It's kind of nice to be small potatoes for once."

Hawk looked up from the menu and grinned, and Laurie was forcefully struck, once again, by the incredible clarity of his eyes. Looking at him, it seemed impossible to her that she could have ever found another face attractive, that there would ever be another she'd enjoy looking at as much as his.

He inclined his head. "What?"

"Nothing." Demurely, she lowered her gaze. "I guess I need to stop mooning at you in public. The tabloids will be filled with the princess's inappropriate liaison with her bodyguard."

He picked up a breadstick. "Oughta be good for my reputation when I get back home."

A knife twisted in her chest, but Laurie forced a smile. "I can imagine." Lightly, she asked, "Will you go back to work on the force?"

"I don't know." The waiter brought their drinks, and Hawk fell silent, leaning back to allow them to be placed. They ordered antipasti and the waiter nodded approval, then left. "I don't know," Hawk repeated, "how much of what I'm feeling is real healing and how much is just being away from everyday life."

The knife cut through a couple of ribs, but Laurie managed a faint smile. "I understand."

"Do you?"

She wasn't sure how to answer, and she was all too aware of the eyes of the diners and servers. "I think I do," she said mildly. "But perhaps this is not the best place for this conversation."

He inclined his head. "Probably right."

She said in Julia's voice, with Julia's smile, "Things always work out for the best."

He shook his head, bitterness around his mouth. "That's such a load of bull."

"You're welcome to your opinion," she said, still in character. "I choose to hold my own view."

To forestall anything more, she bent her head to study the menu, aware of a brittleness around those sliced ribs and determined not to show it. "I think I'm going to have the chicken Marsala. Have you decided?"

Hawk took the cue. "Steak," he said shortly, and tossed the menu down.

Laurie felt her emotions crowding into her throat. "What is it with you?" she said quietly. "When are you going to grow up?"

He had the grace to look ashamed momentarily, but before he could say anything else, Laurie suddenly stood up. "Excuse me a moment, will you?"

She wasn't sure where the ladies' room was, and Julia would know. That single fact upset Laurie more than it should have as she headed blindly toward the back and a small hallway. Surely it was there. A man, obviously one of the many, many immigrants who provided labor around here, was clearing a table and nodded at her. "Good evening," he said formally in heavily accented English. Laurie nodded politely.

The building was old and the hallway was narrow, twisting around what was obviously another establishment, to a shared set of rest rooms at the very back of the building. To make the long walk more pleasant, the walls had been papered with a flocked Victorian-style paper, and old photos and newspapers were hung along the way. Laurie paused to look at some of them, trying to focus on something external rather than the ache in her chest.

She told herself that she was just feeling the echoes of the tornado on the news—they always upset her—

and the exhaustion of being in planes every day for a week. She glared at a picture of a madam in a low-cut corset and told herself that she'd known from the beginning that Hawk Stone was a bad romantic risk and she had no right to get all upset about it now.

It was just that she'd seen so much more of him these past few days, the gentle and good, as well as the sad boy who'd lost his mother too young and would never handle loss well because of it.

She sidled around a man in chef's whites who was talking on a pay phone close to a door to the parking lot. It was propped open to the sweet-smelling evening, and Laurie noticed dimly that it was nearly sunset. How had that happened so fast? She'd read somewhere that the sun went down early in the mountains, but this was rather startling.

Ducking into the quaint, pretty rest room, she washed her hands, wet a paper towel with cold water and pressed it to her forehead and lips, then her eyes, which felt hot with unshed tears. She told herself to be reasonable. Hawk was right. How could either of them know if this was real until they got back to normal life? Maybe she'd realize that her initial impression was right—a man like him was too much trouble.

Obviously, she thought with a scowl. "Get a grip," she said to her reflection. It wouldn't be long now and they'd be done with all the masquerading, all the travel, everything. And if there was anything real between them, they'd know it.

That helped. She squared her shoulders and pulled open the door.

The man on the phone turned and hung up the receiver. Laurie thought he was heading toward the men's room, just beyond the ladies', and stepped sideways to let him by. He stared at her too intently, large dark eyes focused on her face, and she realized he thought she was the princess. She smiled.

Then a cloth was clamped over her mouth and she was jerked backward, and as she raised her hands to pull the gag off and scream, whoever was behind her pinned her arms at her sides roughly. The man who'd been on the phone moved in swiftly, barking out a quick order in Arabic.

Laurie knew one split second of panic—how could she have been so stupid?—before she reacted, bringing her heel down hard on the arch of the man behind her, and swinging forward from the waist to see if she could throw him. Her gun was strapped to her ankle, beneath the loose hem of the khaki slacks, and if she could get her arm free, she could halt this right now.

An elbow or knee caught her nose and mouth, and Laurie felt a lower incisor cut hard into her upper lip, tasted the gush of blood and felt it spilling out of her nose. She grunted, staggering a little to the left in her effort to flip the man behind her off her back. They slammed sideways into the wall, and she saw some of the blood splatter the white tiles on the floor, but she also heard her captor grunt in pain and surprise. He twisted the gag painfully and pulled upward on her elbows, and Laurie recognized they'd be broken if she struggled further. She eased a little, choked on the blood, spent a split-second in regrouping.

The man in front grabbed her ankles, finding the gun strapped there, and growled in surprise as he pulled it out, cinching her knees under his broad arm. It gave her one more chance, and she twisted her body hard and jerked her torso forward. She fell, slamming knees and hip to the ground, breaking the hold of the first man. As soon as she hit the floor, she wiggled toward an opening between them, managing to get to her knees. Her nose was bleeding badly and she choked, trying to pull off the gag and get to her feet at the same time. She staggered sideways when one man made a grab for her, and slammed into the door-jamb. Only one more second and she'd be free.

One of them grabbed her hair, snapping back her head. Laurie gurgled, still attempting to fight her way free, and then the other grabbed her by the waist. They stepped outside, Laurie carried like a sack of potatoes between them. When she struggled, one of them hit her, and she realized that if she was going to get any kind of quarter from them, she had to stop. As her instructor said, there was a time to fight and a time to go with the flow.

She turned her head and let the blood drip out of her nose. It would kill Hawk to see it, but at least it would be something of a clue. They carried her to a plain white sedan, beat-up and anonymous, and loaded her into the trunk, onto a blanket that had obviously been put there for her. She had a moment of panic and raised beseeching eyes to the man who dumped her there, pulling at his arm, making a noise of protest.

He slammed the trunk closed.

As they drove off, Laurie pulled the gag from her mouth and held it to her bleeding nose. For the second time in her life, she was terrified. What if Hawk was right and things didn't always work out?

Hawk sat at the table, wondering when he'd decided he had to be the biggest jerk on the planet at every turn. He'd known Laurie was unsettled by the tornado, and had brought her here to make her feel better, take her mind off of that old trauma.

But something had happened in him when she gave him that look across the table, her eyes shining and full of light, hope making her skin radiant, her love so plain it might as well have been tattooed on her forehead in a little heart: Laurie loves Hawk.

It wasn't that he didn't love her. He just wasn't sure, all of a sudden, that any of this was real. He'd been feeling clearer and happier than he had in months, that was true, but wasn't it like camp or something, where *nothing* was real? Even more so in this case, since he wasn't always sure if he was attracted to a princess or to the woman who was pretending to be her. Which one did he make love to with such abandon?

How could he trust anything about himself or his instincts? That was the bottom line. He'd been second-guessing himself so long that nothing was real or authentic anymore.

When she didn't come back after five minutes, he worried that she might be having a little crying session in the bathroom, and it made him feel guilty and sad and even more confused. He should never have started all this if he couldn't commit to something. He'd known that in the beginning, and had let himself get carried away.

But after ten minutes, he started to get worried.

After fifteen, he was sick, and jumped up to go look for her. He walked down the long hallway, dread building as he realized how far it was. He should have come with her!

Damn. A warning pulse beat in his throat.

He saw the open back door and was already pulling out the cell phone to rouse David and Alex. "They got her," he barked into the phone, his body going cold when he saw the blood on the white tiles. "And they hurt her. Get over here right now."

A layer of ice just below his skin isolated Hawk from all emotion. Within ten minutes, the restaurant was shut down and the scene secured. Within forty-five minutes, the media was already crowding into the area with their vans and flash cams and spotlights, but Hawk, Alex and Dave utilized the local police—who were used to celebrity cases, thank God—to keep the evidence from being tainted.

It was a straightforward scenario. Laurie had been ambushed as she came out of the bathroom, probably by two men. She'd struggled and been wounded. Hawk wondered grimly why she hadn't screamed. He hadn't been far away; he would have heard her.

They followed the blood trail to an empty parking space, and questioned the restaurant staff, who said the two employees who'd gone missing during the incident were new hires, brothers named Mohammed and Nuri Laziz. They drove a white sedan, maybe an eighties model, but no one could remember exactly.

Alex looked grim. "Smart."

Hawk nodded, the ice under his skin making his face muscles too stiff to move.

It turned out that the address they'd given was false. Big surprise. They had not had green cards, and there was no record of a license issued to anyone in those names, nor a car registered to them. Another big surprise.

Hawk relentlessly questioned all the employees, hoping for anything that would tip them off. One young waitress acted a little skittish, and he finally cornered her.

"Hey, honey," he said kindly. "You ever see the princess in here before?"

She shook her head. She was skinny, with big eyes and slightly uneven front teeth. Pretty, but only because she was so young. "I've seen her picture. That's all."

"You ever date either of those guys?"

"Why do you ask me that?"

"Just a question."

She lowered her eyes. "I went out with Nuri a couple of times. He was really nice—took me to have a steak and everything. He's really lonely here." She traced an edge of the bar with her fingernail. "We talk a lot, you know, when it's slow."

"Did he take you home with him, maybe?"

Her cheeks colored. "I wanted him to, but he wouldn't. There were three other guys living with him, he said. We went to my place."

"You don't know where he stayed?"

She shook her head. "I didn't have nothing to do with this, I swear. I didn't know he was a terrorist."

"Did he ever say anything about his beliefs, anything you can think of that would tell us what group he might be affiliated with?"

"Like what?"

"Did he mention the politics of home? Any rulers by name? Anything?"

"Not that I can think of. We didn't really, uh, talk about stuff like that." She frowned, lifted her head. "He wears this thing, though, around his neck. Some kind of symbol.'' Taking a pen out of her pocket, she drew it on a napkin.

The ice thickened an inch. Hawk took the drawing to Alex. ''What's this?''

''Brothers of Darkness,'' he said, and swore.

Chapter 15

Laurie was hustled from the trunk to a cabin. It was dark and she couldn't see much except that they were high in the mountains. There was a chill in the air, and she smelled pine and water as they hauled her out of the trunk, one on either side as they marched her to a small, primitive cabin.

Her stomach roiled a little as they pushed her into the room, speaking with each other in Arabic. Laurie was suddenly afraid of what they might do to her. She thought of the man who'd tried to grab her before, thought of his hands on her breasts, and wondered what the odds were that terrorists would rape a princess.

And how, exactly, did one manage that gracefully? Fight or not? Fight and be raped anyway, and maybe killed, or lie there and think of England?

As it were.

The thought was the faintest bit hysterical, but it

was also a little bit funny. She took a deep breath, steeling herself for whatever might happen, feeling a tenseness in her legs and at the base of her spine. Once inside, she shrugged off the hands that held and shook her arms a little. They had entered a room furnished with nothing but benches and a broad table. Oil lamps burned, dispelling the darkness.

One more man waited inside, obviously the top dog by the way the other two deferred to him, answering questions he shot at them in Arabic. He was tall and broad through the shoulders, with dark eyes so cold they reminded her of marbles.

"Welcome, Princess," he said with irony. "I hope you'll find your stay with us most comfortable."

She didn't answer. Her nose was aching—she was seriously afraid it might be broken—and her stomach was upset from swallowing so much blood. Laurie wasn't sure she had it in her to be the soft-spoken Julia. Better just to be silent rather than give away the charade.

They led her to a small room without windows. A cot and blankets lay on the floor, obviously slept in. Without a word, the door was closed, and she heard a lock slide home from the outside.

Now what? She wished she had a watch. It was hard to gauge time without light, and she knew that time often underwent distortions under the kind of circumstances of danger and trauma she'd just experienced. In some ways, it felt like a couple of years since she'd left the table to go to the rest room, her heart stinging. The picture of herself in the bathroom, nearly in tears, disgusted her now, and she jumped up to pace the four steps from one end of the room to the other.

She'd managed it all very badly. All the training in the world couldn't make up for experience, she realized now. Next time—if they ever let her have another chance—she would have better instincts. She'd keep her gun closer to hand. She'd—

Whatever. She would learn from this.

Her nose throbbed, right across the bridge, like a gnome was pounding out a symphony from the inside, and she couldn't breathe very well through it. Her lip was badly cut, too, and she could tell it was swollen. She pounded on the door and almost said, "Hey!" but remembered in time to stay in character. No matter what happened, she had to do that much. If they found out she wasn't the princess, they'd just kill her and move on.

Or at least she hoped they'd just kill her. Gang rape, then death, didn't sound like a ton of fun. Better just something nice and quick—a bullet to the head should do it.

She pounded again. "Hello!"

The same man who'd led her to the room opened the door. "What?"

"May I have some water?" She remembered, finally, that the princess had a big plus on her side, especially given that these were old-world men. She put her hand over her belly protectively. "I'll do anything you say, but I ask your consideration for my child."

He gave a nod, said something to his boss, evidently obtained approval. The boss said, cutting an apple with a wicked-looking knife, "Give her some bread, too."

The minion went outside and came back carrying a pitcher of water, the sides still wet, along with a purple tin cup and half of a round loaf of bread. "Thank you," she said.

He closed and locked the door once again.

One of Laurie's goals in getting them to open the door had been to get a clearer idea of the layout of the cabin, but it wasn't encouraging. Only one door that she could see. A pair of high windows, too narrow to climb through. It was a hunting cabin of some sort, obviously, meant to offer shelter and little more.

The water tasted clean and fresh, but she couldn't tell anything about it, which she had hoped to do. It was only good clean water—which could even have been drawn from a stream or creek this high up, before water had a chance to be polluted. She thought of giardia with a little wince, but drank it anyway. It helped to settle her stomach. She found it difficult to chew the bread well, partly because the tooth that had cut her lip kept scraping the tenderest spot, but also because she needed to breathe through her mouth, and wasn't all that simple to breathe and eat at the same time. Still, she managed to get it all down, a small bite at a time, not sure when she would have more. Better to be prepared.

Then there was nothing to do but sit in the dark. Beyond the door, the kidnappers were quiet, talking only sporadically. One had a cell phone that rang twice, and it struck Laurie as absurd that a trio of rough terrorists had a sleek, silvery cell phone that rang like the first bars of Beethoven's "F'aur Elise." She imagined they were arranging ransom.

With a sigh, she lay down and pulled the blanket over her shoulders. Food and water would keep her going, but sleep would be a good idea, too. Even if she figured a way out tonight, which was unlikely since it was pitch-dark in the room, she wouldn't be able to find her way through the forest at night.

Because of the long day, because she'd been so tired for the past two days, she fell asleep almost instantly, thinking just before she drifted off that it was a great blessing. A way out of anything.

At midnight, Hawk paced the living area of the business-style hotel room where Alex and Dave had been put up, surprised by the sterility of it after so much luxury. A command center had been set up on the table, and cords snaked from the wall to various pieces of machinery. A computer was plugged into a modem line and a man with a gray buzz cut took command of it, his hairy fingers tapping quickly to secure the line and make contact with the databases in Washington. Harold Peterson was his name, and he reminded Hawk of his father in some way he couldn't pinpoint. Other agents talked on phones, and someone else monitored some machine Hawk had never seen before.

He didn't care what it did.

The ice that had been shielding him at first now melted, one layer at a time. He felt the protection going and paced the length of the room again, his mind racing. How could they find her? Where was she right now? How badly was she hurt? He had a roaring need to do something, anything, other than sit here and let the night pass.

The night. The long, endless hours of night.

Every time he thought about the blood spots leading in a trail to the empty parking space, he felt a tremor of rage rising in him again. Scuff marks in the hallway showed a struggle—and he thought of her in the training room, fiercely fighting a heavier, stockier man with good results. But the truth was the assailants had succeeded in abducting her.

The agents had sent out emergency bulletins on the news and to the newspapers, offering substantial rewards for information that would lead to the capture of the terrorists, and the scanner ran all night with police calls. Hawk listened intently, thinking of Laurie's joke about people who fretted over scanners. Right now, all he wanted was a break. The local cops were out in droves, canvassing every neighborhood, checking campgrounds where hordes of service personnel set up villages because housing was too expensive. Police traveled down to smaller communities in the area, asking in bars and coffee shops for information on the brothers.

Nothing had turned up so far. It had been five hours, and nothing. Hawk's neck was tight, his chest ached and his eyes burned from staring at the intelligence they collected in tiny bits, hoping they'd fit together into some kind of pattern.

He was furious with himself for not accompanying her to the ladies' room. It was a prime example of why emotional involvements were a bad idea on the job—things on a personal level had been tense enough that Hawk had attributed her absence to the backwash of a lover's quarrel, instead of keeping the assignment front and center where it belonged.

Just as he had the night in Dallas. He'd reacted to her scream, then to her injuries, not like a partner but a lover. A big mistake.

Alex looked up. "Why don't you catch a few winks, man?"

Hawk tried not to see the sympathy in his eyes.

"I'm all right," he growled, and went back to pacing, going over and over the pieces of information they'd collected. The trouble was, he wasn't on home ground now. All the things that made him good at tracking suspects in Flagstaff were useless here, and he had no choice but to let the beat cops do their thing.

In frustration, he sat down at the table and picked up a sheaf of papers—reports and neighborhood surveys and transcripts of phone calls. It all blurred together under the force of a headache, and he put it down with a sigh.

Maybe Alex was right. He should catch a few winks. Be fresh when dawn came. He stretched out on the couch and closed his eyes.

As a child, he'd been prone to night terrors, even before his mother died. She'd sometimes sung to him, chasing away the monsters under his bed with a broom, leaving a light burning all night if he needed it. When she died, he'd been unable to sleep well for more than a year, unable to tell his auntie that he needed monsters banished. At last she had come to him one night with a hot cup of some freshly brewed medicinal tea, and made him drink it while she told him stories—old stories about the world and new stories about people in the family. She'd told him about her mother, his own grandmother, who had said there was a place in everybody that was still and quiet and safe, that anyone could go there whenever they wanted. Hawk's aunt showed him how to go there that night, and he'd practiced, faithfully, until he could go at will.

It had been little help to him in recent months, but tonight he was desperate and tried it again. He saw himself in the desert on a cloudy morning, the gray-

ness softening the harsh shadows of cactus and sage,
and felt a cool wind blowing, easing the heat on his
skin. He breathed it in, the smell of desert and morning, fresh and untainted by anything human. And with
him, sitting by a fire, was his mother, her long braid
falling over her shoulder.

He knew he was dreaming as soon as he saw her,
because she didn't usually figure into the visualiza-
tions. Still, he was happy to see her, and sat down.
"Mom! I am so glad to see you."

She fed twigs to the fire and smiled. "I can come
anytime."

In the way of dreamers, Hawk said, "I didn't know
that, but of course it's true." He frowned. "Why are
you here now?"

"To let you ask me whatever you want."

Hawk thought for a moment. "Is she okay?"

His mother looked troubled. "For now."

Urgency tightened his pectoral muscles. "How
long do we have?"

His mother looked at the fire and inclined her head,
as if she was listening. "One day."

"And how do I find where she is?"

"Listen to the old man."

Hawk jerked awake violently. He had no idea how
long it had been that he'd slept, but he saw that Alex
was stretched out in a chair, his feet in front of him,
snoring. Only the old guy at the computer was still at
it, his fingers tapping, flying, stopping, then tapping
again.

Hawk poured a drink of water. "What do you
have?"

"Dossiers. This is a nasty group." He pulled up
mug shots of the two brothers, and Hawk recognized

the busboy immediately. They both had rap sheets with a host of petty terrorist crimes, and were suspected of another list that was a lot more terrifying.

Peterson clicked the mouse. "I'm guessing this guy is with them, too. We're looking for three men, not two."

A face with the hard eyes of a statue came up. He was older than the others, his mouth grim.

"Amin Qadir," Peterson said. "Widely thought to be a major source of funding for Brothers of Darkness. He's the twenty-third son of a sheik, well educated, skilled in languages, a little rough around the edges because his mother was cast out due to a love affair." He clicked some more. "She was lucky she wasn't killed," he said, almost to himself. "The sheik must have been fond of her."

Hawk leaned forward, something niggling at the edges of his brain. His mother had said to listen to the old man, and while Hawk didn't think she had really appeared to him in his dream, he suspected it was his subconscious's way of getting his attention, helping him see what he'd missed.

"Is there anything from an old man in here? The stuff that came in today, I mean?"

David, coming out of the kitchen with a Dagwood sandwich, said, "There was that old mountain man. Came into town when he heard the police calls on the radio."

Hawk straightened. "What'd he say?" He reached for the stack of papers on the table. "Did they take a statement?"

"Nah. The local cops say he shows up all the time at crime scenes, carrying his rifle." He chewed, grinning around the sandwich. "Should have seen him—beard to his waist, I swear. Just like a cartoon."

"Who talked to him?" Hawk asked.

"Alex, then that skinny white cop. Johnson? Kennedy. It was Kennedy."

Hawk picked up the phone and dialed police headquarters. "This is Hawk Stone from the FBI," he said to the dispatcher. "I need to page Officer Kennedy immediately."

Laurie woke up one excruciating inch at a time. It was a headache, actually, that pulled her out of the downy well of sleep—the worst headache she could ever remember having. It almost seemed to have noise with it. She tried to breathe, but her nasal passages were obviously swollen, and she had to take a breath through her mouth, which she must have been doing all night, because her throat was dry as a bone.

Before she moved, she catalogued everything. First herself. The headache. Check. Really roaring, but not debilitating—if she could think through it, which at the moment seemed questionable. The rest of her body felt a little bruised and stressed, but no worse than if she'd had a good workout at the dojo the day before.

But she was cold and hungry and thirsty.

Beyond the closed door was a slice of light, and Laurie thought it looked more like daylight than the flickering orangish color of the lanterns. If it was daylight, she might be able to figure out some way to get out of here. The water she'd smelled the night before might have been a lake, but it could be a stream, and that would be a big help. Water nearly always led to civilization. If she followed it long enough. Nor would she dehydrate on a walk like that.

But how to get past the terrorists?

She heard them talking in the other room, in ordinary conversational tones. She thought she smelled coffee, but wasn't quite sure. And come to that, maybe the water scent last night had been an illusion, too, an illusion based on wishful thinking. How could she have smelled anything?

She remembered that she'd smelled pine. Okay, so it was a trustworthy sense.

Pull yourself together.

The command came from deep inside her brain, some clear voice telling her to stop having this debate with herself about smells and figure something out. What? What advantage did she have that these men did not have? They were taller, strong and obviously not afraid of hurting her. They were armed. They guarded the door. They knew where they were and she didn't.

What else? She sat up slowly, and discovered her head hurt no more in that position than it had when she was lying down. What else?

She was not really the princess. She was a woman. She was much stronger and better prepared than they believed.

The princess. Julia. Julia. Julia…

The baby.

Of course. If you got right down to it, these were guys. Nothing was guaranteed to scare her brothers more than a pregnant woman who might be in trouble. They were almost superstitious about it. She almost smiled.

With a loud moan, she doubled over and started to

cry. "Help me!" She moaned again, rolling back and forth on the blanket. "Help!"

Almost immediately the one she thought of as The Younger appeared. "What is it?"

Laurie rolled and mimed retching, holding her head and her belly at the same time. "Please, I am so ill. Help me." Her hand shook as she reached out to him. "Please. I do not want to lose my baby!"

He backed away, horrified, and Laurie saw through the narrow high windows that it was indeed daylight. Very early. He spoke something in Arabic to the other two, pointing at her, and they all three stared at the door with something like terror. An argument of some sort ensued, and Laurie struggled to her feet, not having to pretend all that much to be staggering and in pain as she made her way forward. "Please," she said, holding her belly.

They kept on arguing. Laurie could see they were bickering over who should accompany her, and although she'd put her hopes on The Younger, at last it was the second man who'd nabbed her who threw down a spoon and stood up. He looked over his shoulder once and the boss nodded, his lips pinched. The Older inclined his head toward the door. Laurie extended her hand. "I cannot."

Looking pale, he came forward, and Laurie put her hand on his arm, leaning hard and shaking like a very old woman as she took tentative steps into the room. She focused on her headache, and discovered that the dizziness was not an act—every slight jarring of her head made her feel slightly faint and nauseous.

All the way across the cabin she kept up the act, trying to decide exactly how to use this situation once she got outside and into a position to run. It had to be good when she made the break. She wouldn't get a second chance. She gripped the man's arm tightly, testing the tensility of his muscles, and she could sense him pulling away.

A few more steps to the door. Outside, oblivious to the drama, a chorus of birds chirped and twittered a greeting to the day. As Laurie stepped outside, she had to blink at the brightness—buttery gold light sparkling on aspen leaves and dappling the earth beneath them. It made her headache worse.

The latrine was dead ahead, a narrow shack with slits cut in the sides. Seeing it, Laurie realized she most urgently needed to avail herself of the facilities within, and it would be extremely difficult to mount a good escape under those circumstances.

It seemed like a ridiculous problem to face. Not a gun or a knife or the fate of the free world, just how to get away when one had a very full bladder. What did all those tough agents do when they needed to use the bathroom?

She stumbled a little, moaning for effect, trying to buy a little time. Somewhere close by was a river or stream—she could hear it, sense the ions in the air. Her captor started muttering under his breath, and she thought it might be singsong enough to be a prayer.

Her head cleared a little. What did one do? The necessary. Top priority in this instant was the rest room. Then she'd figure out the rest.

A little flash of something caught her eye to the east and she looked up, feeling her escort tense along with her. She frowned, seeing nothing, but the hairs on the back of her neck prickled. A little hope rose in her. Maybe she wouldn't have to do this all alone, after all.

A traitorous voice rose in the back of her mind, taunting her. *Oh, looking for a rescue? Can't handle the tough work, after all?*

Laurie set her mouth and very nearly spoke aloud. *I'll take all the help I can get.*

Officer Kennedy—it was a good omen that he shared a name with Laurie's brother, Hawk thought— paged headquarters within ten minutes. The complaint by the old man had been a typical rant—he was tired of all the foreigners taking over the mountains, not paying taxes properly while he had to pay too damned much for anything. "He's an old-timer," Kennedy explained. "Been here since before property values skyrocketed. He's probably sitting on a million dollars worth of land up there, but he's always in a fight with the government about something or another. Real character. He shows up on nearly every case we get."

Hawk pursed his lips. He was familiar with the type. Most cops knew one or more. "I hear you," he said. "Is there any chance he might really know something this time? Does he always talk about foreigners? Did he give any details?"

"With all due respect, you're barking up the wrong tree."

"She's my partner. Better to chase a dead end than sit here with nothing to do."

"Yeah, okay. I'll buy that. You can chase him down. I've got an address—we'll swing by and take you on up there."

"Now?"

Kennedy snorted a little. "Yeah, why the hell not? The old man'll kiss you for listening. He'll be thrilled."

It was nearly morning when they arrived, but when Hawk and the two other officers stepped out of the car in front of a sturdily built stone cottage, the old man stood on the porch. Hawk saw immediately that he wasn't the kind of loose cannon he was used to. There were neat curtains hung at the windows, and the old man did have a long beard, but his hair had been cut recently. His clothes were clean and ordinary—jeans, a T-shirt with an advertising slogan for beer over the chest, heavy boots. He did have a rifle in his hands, but out here that probably wasn't all that unusual.

Hawk nodded. "Morning, Mr. Sutter. I'm with the FBI and I'd like to talk to you if you have a minute."

"What's this about? My taxes are done paid, curse the blasted IRS."

"No, sir." Hawk gestured to the officers as he approached the porch. He stopped at the stairs, put one foot on the lower step, and forced himself to adopt a casual attitude. "Kennedy here tells me you might have some information about some Arabs that kidnapped Princess Julia."

He nodded sadly. "I know where they are. I'da tried myself, but three to one and me s'old—well, not even an old mountain man's got *huevos* that big, if you know what I mean."

"We have to be careful, as you can imagine, so we don't get in trouble with the bosses." Hawk rolled his eyes discreetly.

The old man harrumphed.

"You think you can lead us there?"

"Hell, yes. Just over that rise there. It's a hunting cabin for some big shot outta L.A., but I ain't got no claim on the land, so I mind my own business. How'd I know he didn't make friends with some prince or something?"

"I can respect that. I'd like to ask you, what made you think of these men when you heard about the abduction?"

"They're A-rabs. I heard 'em singing one morning, when I was out with my dogs. Saw 'em in the yard, bowing and scraping, and once you've seen that, you don't forget." With a lift of his chin, he added, "I was in Egypt back in World War II, you know."

Hawk swallowed his sense of urgent impatience. Hurrying an old man wasn't something he could do, and it wouldn't do any good, anyway. "Is that right? I'd really like to hear more about that sometime. My great-uncle served in Italy. Told me a whole lot of stories." He brushed an invisible bit of dust from his shirt. "Was there anything else these guys did that made you think they might not just be on vacation up here or something?"

"They got a lotta guns, son. Other things I don't much like the look of, too." He set his mouth. "If they ain't your guys, they're up to no good, anyhow."

Hawk glanced over his shoulder at the other officers. Kennedy was standing straighter. He nodded, shifted his head toward the rise the old man had indicated. Hawk turned back. "How far is it?"

"Not ten minutes." Sutter looked at the sky. "Daybreak'll be here in no time. You all might as well come in and have a cup of coffee first."

"That'd be great," Hawk said. "We'll radio for a little backup, eh?"

"Not a bad idea." The old-timer paused midstep. "If these are your men, think there'll be a reward in it for an old man?"

Hawk smiled, thinking of the princess's private jet. "I bet we can come up with something for you." He clapped him on the shoulder. "Let's have some of that coffee."

It was closer to forty-five minutes before the team was fully assembled, a SWAT team in full combat dress, what felt like half the local police force and the full team of FBI. Hawk was impressed with how quickly they moved—and took his instructions to lead the team as if it were only obvious who should do so.

Sutter led them up a rise along a narrow but well-worn path, and near the top of a ridge, halted. "Might want to tell them all to hold back just now," he said to Hawk. "We'll go forward and you can see for yourself the lay of the land. It's a bit of a hollow, with the stream down front."

Hawk nodded and gave the signal. He and the old man hiked to the crest of the hill and looked down.

The cabin sat against a wall of rock, the stream in front, a latrine to one side. Beneath a tree was parked the white sedan they'd sought, and Hawk set his jaw.

No emotion. Only the job.

Smoke puffed out of a chimney pipe—probably from a wood stove. The place was crude, with no entry but the front door, and narrow high windows. It wasn't designed to be secure, just warm, but the end result was the same—a fact the terrorists had no doubt used to their advantage. The stream offered possibilities of penetration, and it would be possible to surround the hollow, but that strategy was only useful if they were willing to sacrifice the victim.

Not an option.

Hawk's gaze went back to the latrine. Sooner or later, someone would need it. The team would wait to strike until then. "Good work," he said to Sutter. He was about to turn back down the hill when the cabin door opened and two figures came out. His heart froze for an agonizing second as he saw Laurie, stumbling and obviously sick, being led to the outhouse.

He raised his hand in a signal, directing the troops to fan out. It was too damned quiet on the mountain to risk radio contact, and they couldn't be sure the waves wouldn't be picked up. They'd just have to make the best of this opportunity. He bent down and untied his shoes.

He was going in.

Chapter 16

The world narrowed to one thing, an utterly silent descent down a very steep hillside. It had to be done quickly. Hawk saw Laurie stumble into the latrine, and he was already moving, dancing like the child who'd learned at a dozen powwows how to leap lightly, when to make the bells and rattles make noise and when to keep them still. He had more weight on him now, and a forest wasn't a smooth gymnasium floor, but it worked for him anyway. He used the trees as cover and landed lightly on smooth ground, making no noise that could be heard over the din of birds.

The cabin door was closed, a streak of good fortune, and Hawk closed in from behind, his arm tight around the man's neck, his hand over his mouth before he even knew what hit him. Three other agents, equally silent, came up behind him and secured the suspect. A burly cop covered his mouth with a beefy hand, and the man's terrified eyes showed he was truly caught.

The latrine door swung open, and Hawk jumped forward, putting his hand over Laurie's mouth, too, before she could react in any way to the scene. He saw the mess of her face, felt a prickling of emotion and clamped down on it hard. She nodded, letting him know she understood, and he let his hand down.

"Oh, man, I'm glad to see you," she whispered.

"How many inside?"

"Two. Four guns is what I saw, but there might be more."

"Good work." He cocked his head. "Now get out of the way."

She didn't argue, as he half thought she might, and Hawk forgot her as the team came down the hillside at his signal. They surrounded the cabin, assault rifles at the ready, and waited for word. He took the bullhorn offered to him by an FBI agent, and started to use it.

The door opened and a man in an undershirt appeared, still talking to someone over his shoulder. He turned, saw Hawk and raised a gun, shouting something in Arabic. As the man fired, Hawk ducked, hitting the dirt and tossing the bullhorn away. He steadied his own gun, aimed and fired cleanly—right through the knee.

The man screamed and fell, and the other agents swarmed into the cabin over him, coming out in less than a minute with a tall, well-built man who almost casually held his hands behind his head. Across the short space, Hawk met his eyes and saw that the man knew he'd be free in no time, that he had connections that wouldn't let him be kept in this country.

And with a certain satisfaction, Hawk smiled.

They'd see about that.

Huddled in a blanket in an ambulance twenty minutes later, Laurie drank a hot cup of coffee with more gratitude than was seemly. She'd drunk a liter of water in about five seconds flat before she'd even let them look at her, then allowed the paramedics to check her over. "I swear, it's all in my face," she said repeatedly.

It turned out she also had what they suspected were broken ribs beneath the clear imprint of a boot. "Hmm," she said with surprise. "I didn't even feel that one."

The medic gave her a cock-eyed grin. "Damn, girl, maybe you oughta take up boxing. I know grown men who'd be crying about all this." He winced as he washed her face. "The nose is definitely broken, and I don't know that it's ever gonna be perfect again."

She lifted a shoulder. "What good is a perfect nose—except for the occasional princess gig?"

He chuckled, shaking his head. "Let's get you to town for some X rays, huh?"

"Can I run the siren?" Laurie asked, tongue in cheek.

He looked up, saw that she was kidding and said, "Sure, honey. Whatever tickles your fancy."

Laurie looked anxiously out the back of the ambulance for Hawk, feeling a little nervous that he hadn't had much to say to her after their initial contact. She told herself that was silly, that he was busy securing the scene, directing personnel, collecting evidence.

But she ached to put her head on his shoulder for

just one minute. It had been a very, very long twelve hours, and beneath her facade she felt unsteady and exhausted. "Would you mind if we waited a few more minutes?" she asked.

"Hey, honey, we're here for you."

She nodded. "Hang on then. I'll be right back."

With as much dignity as she could muster, considering how she probably looked—like a cat dragged over about five miles of muddy roads, she figured, not that she'd let anyone give her a mirror—she waded into the thicket of men. Hawk was giving directions to a forensics team, particular details about what he needed for the FBI and how the investigation should be directed. Knowing he saw her, she waited until he finished. "Can I talk to you for a minute?"

She sensed his hesitance more than saw it: a brief pause, a shift of his body away from her, as if he would run, the slight twitch of a muscle in his jaw. "Sure."

He came forward, putting his hand on the small of her back as he had done so many times before, and led her to a quiet spot beneath a tree. He didn't quite meet her eyes. "You okay?"

"Like you care," she heard herself say. "You big fat jerk."

He lifted his head. "What?"

"Were you ever gonna get around to finding out if I was really okay?"

He closed his eyes. "Laurie, I'm trying to be professional here." His jaw went hard and he opened his eyes to meet her gaze. "They're all talking about you, how tough you are—taking broken ribs like nothing, a broken nose with no tears. You'll be in the field full-time." He paused. "But not if they know we've been involved. It's a credibility problem for both of us, you understand?''

She stared at him. ''I don't know that I do understand, Hawk. Is it over between us, then?''

He licked his bottom lip. ''I know what you want, Laurie, and you've earned it.''

''Do you really know, Hawk?'' she asked in a level tone. ''Do you?''

He bowed his head. ''I'll come over to the hospital, when there aren't so many guys around, okay? We'll talk then.'' He reached out his fingers and brushed the back of her hand. ''Give me an hour or two to get used to looking at you without wanting to kill somebody, huh?''

She sighed. ''Fine.''

It was agony to look at her, but Hawk forced himself to do it. Both eyes were ringed with dark red-and-purple bruises, and the bridge of her nose was red and swollen. Her lower lip had a gash that likely should have had a stitch or two, and was twice its normal size. An angry scratch ran down her throat, and the clothes were a mess. The paramedic had told him she'd broken a couple of ribs, too.

And he'd heard the talk among the other agents within minutes—how she'd done a hell of a job here. Who knew the sweet little agent from Nebraska had it in her to be so tough?

She'd done it. Proved to all of them—including Hawk—that she had what it took to be a good field agent. She could do it all the time now if she so chose, take on new assignments filled with risk to life and limb. Challenge tough guys, carry a gun, travel into danger in exotic places.

He swallowed. "I'm proud of you," he said roughly. "I want everything for you that you want for yourself, I really do." He resisted the urge to put his hand on her hair. "You've given me back all the things I thought were lost, and in return, I'm gonna step back and let you go on to that life you've been working so hard to get."

She rolled her eyes, and it was almost comical, given the destruction of her face.

Somehow, his big speech wasn't going over all that well. Weren't women supposed to melt when you said things like that? Wasn't that what they all wanted? "Hawk, if you want to run away, go right ahead. Run back to that reservation and your horses and your lonely life, but don't blame it on me, you got it?"

Bad to worse. "I'm not blaming you."

"Have you ever seen the *Sound of Music,* Hawk?"

"Sure. Everybody has."

"I'm going to go to the hospital now and get my X rays, and then I'm going back to the Sebastiani cabin to sleep for about a hundred years. Don't you even think about joining me until you remember the song Julie Andrews and Christopher Plummer sing to each other in that gazebo. Got it?"

"I don't remember it, Laurie. Just tell me."

"Nope. No deal." She sighed and shook her head, pushing away from the tree and from him. "Men are such idiots," she said, and walked her purely American, healthy, confident walk. Half the men there stopped what they were doing to watch her, and she knew it and didn't mind. In spite of his bewilderment and the slight distancing that went along with a crime scene for him, he was proud as hell of her. He thought back to the night he met her in the FBI offices in D.C.

and realized how much she'd gained, even as his heart was breaking.

He wouldn't see her again. His confidence in himself had been restored, and his father had been right to pair him with Laurie, who'd given him back the color in his world, renewed his sense of himself. He'd even handled the scene with his old expertise, without faltering as he'd been half afraid he would.

But even with all of that, he knew he couldn't stand the agony of worrying about her twenty-four hours a day. He'd lost enough in his life. He didn't choose to put himself in a position to lose anymore.

Laurie was fuming by the time she got back to the Sebastiani cabin. Her heart was broken and she was shaky from having too little food and too much excitement in the past twenty-four hours. And in truth, she was also a little giddy. She had succeeded!

She asked the cook to make some sandwiches and bring them to her room, where she stripped off her clothes gratefully and padded into the bathroom to take a shower. Beneath her skin buzzed a little whirl of post-event excitement, and she couldn't quite come down. She kept thinking of Hawk. Wishing he was here. Wishing that—

Oh, she'd just expected the ending of this to be so different! She'd wanted him to greet her with wild kisses, with his hands in her hair and declarations of undying love on his lips. Instead, she'd received pure Hawk: confusion and honor wrapped up in one complex human being. His hands brushing close to her, betraying his need to touch her; his eyes, pleading with her to understand; his mouth saying all the wrong things, with him thinking they were right.

She heaved a sigh. He was just such a *man*.

It had clearly upset him to look at her. And before the bathroom filled entirely with steam, she told herself she had to finally face the damages—what had happened to her.

With a big fluffy towel, she wiped the mirror clean and faced herself.

It was bad. Her stomach swooped oddly as she stared at her almost unrecognizable face in the mirror. Her eyes were black; both her mouth and her nose were swollen. Little bruises and scratches littered her neck and shoulders. The bruises from the mauling in Dallas were still visible, and she had tape on her broken ribs.

She thought of her terror, and the worry that she would be raped and her fear that she wouldn't be able to handle it. She thought of fighting as hard as she could, with all her considerable talent, and losing anyway. She thought of that grim dark room and the complete disregard of her kidnappers.

She let herself cry.

It wasn't so much that she had done badly. She felt a lot of pride, actually, that she'd done as well as she had. She'd kept the princess safe, and managed everything that happened. She'd had a chance to test herself, and had passed the test.

But in the end, she thought field work would be a lot like tornadoes. The threat of violence would always exist. It might come from anywhere, at any moment, and part of the game was in learning to live with that threat.

Laurie could not.

She'd lied about her reasons for escaping Nebraska: overly protective parents and siblings, a bigger world, a chance to figure out who she was. But the truth was, at its heart, very simple. She'd left the Midwest because she couldn't tolerate the thought of ever experiencing another tornado in her life. She didn't like feeling afraid. She liked to be in control. A tornado removed all pretense. It reduced life to a random set of weather conditions that could bubble up at any time, with any variety of results.

Field work would be just like that. Random events could whirl out of control at any second, just as they had with this assignment. She'd been lucky this time. She might have been able to figure out a plan, and had had a good one in place to escape, but if it had not been for Hawk's timely arrival, she might have been a lot more unlucky.

She couldn't live like that. All these years she'd been dreaming of something that would never make her happy. She wept a little for the loss of that dream, then dried her eyes and got in the shower. She'd learned so much, she thought. She'd be even better at the job she'd been doing; maybe she could attain another promotion within a year. Make more money, keep more agents safer, run things from this side and leave the tough work to tougher folk.

It finally didn't seem like such a bad thing to be the nice one, the good girl, the one who took meals to shut-ins and taught Sunday school. It seemed, finally, like the right thing—for her.

And maybe for Hawk.

He was just like her, in a way. A really kindhearted, honest man who'd been blindsided more than once by life's terrible blows. He'd lost his mother, then his partner, and he struggled with it the way any kind, softhearted person would.

Hawk wasn't tough, either. He was masculine and strong and smart, but he had a heart as soft as a marshmallow and probably didn't need to be in the middle of danger and threats any more than she did. They'd both proved they could do it when required, and they'd both picked up the message somewhere that it was important to be tough and in control. But at heart, he was the man who read to her from a scientist's gentle ruminations of life. He was the gentle man who held her hand all day long. He was the one who loved Appaloosas because they had human eyes.

Of course he'd been letting her go. He hadn't wanted to stand in the way of what she'd said over and over was her dream.

In excitement, she turned off the water and pulled the heavy thick towel from over the door to wrap around herself. She would go find him, insist that he listen to her—

He was standing by the door in the bathroom, his arms crossed.

"What do you want?" Laurie asked with a scowl.

He lifted a shoulder. "Thought you might be interested in knowing what they're going to do."

She raised an eyebrow, keeping the towel clutched around her tightly. The rat.

"They're going to send a man in to infiltrate the Brothers of Darkness."

Intrigued in spite of herself, Laurie said, "Who?"

"Walker James. Evidently an international spy of some reputation."

"I've heard of him. Good." She crossed her arms over her chest. "Is there anything else?"

For a minute, he said nothing. His face was inscrutable. Then he took a breath and nodded. "I got it," he said. "The song from the *Sound of Music*. I remembered it." He started to hum it, that sweet, sentimental song about loving someone and feeling blessed because of it. "You love me."

She let herself smile a little. "And you love me."

He took a breath, closed his eyes. "I do, Laurie." He came to her, put his arms around her and let that breath go. "I do. It sounds crazy, considering how long we've known each other and how strange the circumstances are, but I've never known such a strong, pure, honest feeling for anyone in my life. I just want to be with you."

"Me, too," she squeaked. Everything in her melted into his embrace, the one thing she'd been longing for since the kidnappers had taken her the evening before. Fighting off tears of relief, she rested her head in the crook of his shoulder. "I don't want to be a field agent, Hawk. The cost is too great."

He stroked her hair. "Thank God."

"But I don't want to leave the FBI. I want to be in Washington."

"We can work that out." He rocked her a little, side to side. "I've been talking to my father, and he wants to give me a job in security at this... organization he's part of."

Laurie raised her head. "Organization?"

"Top secret. Peacekeeping. They call themselves the Noble Men." He shook his head with a little smile. "He really is a mercenary."

"Are you sure you'll be happy away from the desert, Hawk? Away from all those touchstones?"

"I'm sure," he said, and kissed her. "As long as you love me, I don't care where I live." With a little lift of his shoulder, he added, "It'll be good to live close to my father again, too. I miss him. He's a good guy."

"Yes," she said, thinking with a smile of Caleb Stone's machinations to get them together. "He really is."

And then there was nothing but the two of them, melding together in a kiss that turned not to sex, but to laughter. A laughter tinged with lemons and sunshine and the toughness of two gentle hearts, finally united.

* * * * *

Next month, look for

BORN IN SECRET

by Kylie Brant
as Intimate Moments' riveting
FIRSTBORN SONS
series continues.

Turn the page for a sneak preview...

Chapter 1

At heart, Walker James would always remain a thief. The acknowledgment brought him no shame. He'd been a damn good one in his delinquent youth. If his illegal career had been cut short by Dirk Longfield's interference, well, the talents he'd acquired along the way had been equally useful in the alternative path he'd chosen. Or perhaps, he mused sardonically, it had chosen him. It was doubtful that many people made the conscious decision to become a spy.

He prowled Dirk's well-appointed office, his well-muscled frame moving soundlessly. For once he failed to be amused by his mentor's choice in collectibles. A Ming dynasty vase stood side by side with a chipped and faded replica of Mickey Mouse. A Picasso adorned one wall, hanging next to a scarlet sunset painted on velvet, artist unknown. Beneath his feet was a rich, faded tapestry rug dating from the regime of Catherine the Great. And behind the acre-long walnut desk was a well-known wall hanging of canines cheating at poker.

The rare beside the common. The tacky and the priceless. The collection invited a guest to make all manner of judgments about the collector. They would likely all be wrong. After ten years of friendship with Dirk, Walker knew the man acquired chiefly for whimsy. The value of an object meant far less to him than the fact that it had caught his fancy. Walker didn't share the sentiment, but he understood it. Just as he understood the man who had currently been keeping him waiting for—he checked his watch again—twenty minutes.

The door opened then and he turned a jaundiced eye toward the man strolling toward him. "For a guy who was in such a hurry to get me here, you seem to have developed a sluggish sense of time."

Dirk merely shot him a good-natured smile and clapped an arm around his shoulders. "You're looking good, kid." He reared back, pretended to study the younger man's face. "A few more lines, maybe, but you needed to toughen up that pretty-boy face of yours."

An unwilling smile tugging at his lips, Walker returned the man's embrace. "It's only been three months. I couldn't have aged that much." If he had he would count it as a blessing. The movie star good looks he'd been cursed with at birth didn't exactly make his an anonymous face. That was a damn nuisance in his line of work.

Waving the younger man to a chair; Dirk seated himself. "You probably should have. The way I hear it, you barely managed to escape your last mission with all your limbs intact.'' His casual tone didn't quite mask the concern in his voice.

Walker shrugged. "Let's just say I have a renewed respect for explosives.'' Although he hadn't walked away from the job unscathed, he *had* walked away. It was an important distinction. "The mission was successful."

Dirk's mouth quirked. "I never doubted it. Which leads me, indirectly, to why you're here. I have a job to propose, one that calls for the best. Naturally I thought of you."

"I learned from the best." Walker's quiet answer was more than just factual. It was Dirk who had introduced him to the shadowy world of espionage...a world where right and wrongs weren't always black-and-white, but more often a mottled shade of gray. He'd found it a comfortable enough fit.

Inclining his head to acknowledge the compliment, Dirk went on. "How much have you heard about the trouble brewing between Montebello and Tamir?"

"In which decade?" Walker asked dryly. The two small Middle Eastern countries had been feuding on and off for more than a century. "Seems like I heard something recently about Sheik Ahmed Kamal's son being missing and him accusing King Marcus Sebastiani of responsibility."

Dirk's expression was serious. "Turns out that the king's oldest daughter is pregnant by Kamal's son, Rashid. He was last seen in the company of the princess, so when he came up missing Kamal immediately blamed Sebastiani. The sheik threatened to retaliate by taking over Montebello."

Walker let out a soft, tuneless whistle. Since Montebello was located in a strategic military location, the ramifications were clear. "So the U.S. wants to protect their interests there, discreetly of course, while keeping the peace."

"Partially." Dirk hesitated for a moment, seemed to choose his words carefully. "There have been threats on Sebastiani's family—bombings, attempted kidnappings—and the king believed Kamal was behind them. New intelligence indicates that the sheik wasn't responsible at all, but a rebel faction housed in Maloun called the Brothers of Darkness."

"I've heard of them. They're rumored to have at least one terrorist cell here in the states, near L.A." He frowned, searching his memory. "Seems there was something recently about a UCLA scientist being questioned about a possible connection with them."

"Dr. Sinan Omer. He's suspected of taking a shot at Princess Christina Sebastiani while at a conference out there. We think the Brothers have been heightening the strife between the two countries as a cover. Our sources in the Mideast tell us the organization is close to developing an anthrax virus to use against Kamal's people. They intend to overthrow the sheik's government and bring their own leader into power there."

"Biological warfare." Saying the words, Walker felt chilled. If the organization succeeded, he doubted they'd be content with oil rich Tamir. The entire Middle Eastern world would be at risk. The repercussions would be felt around the world.

He looked at Dirk. "What do I do?" That simply, that easily, he was committed. He could think of nothing he wouldn't do for this man.

The older man looked pleased and a bit relieved. "Before I go into the whole plan, I should tell you that you'll be paired with a partner. I was briefing her before you arrived. I'll get her so we can all discuss the job together.''

Before Walker could respond, Dirk strode to the door, pulled it open and disappeared. Walker rose, stared after the man, something about his behavior striking him as odd. There had been an almost furtive quality to it, which was ludicrous. Dirk had never been anything but up front with him.

Hearing a sound at the door, he turned and stared in disbelief at the woman accompanying the older man. Fate, he'd always thought, was merely the acts of a whimsical god. And right now that god was having a good hard laugh at Walker's expense.

''What's she doing here?'' His voice was flat. He was afraid, very much afraid, that he already knew the answer to that particular question.

His fear was confirmed when Dirk skirted his gaze and said, just a shade too heartily, ''You remember Jasmine, of course. She'll be your partner on this case.''

Walker glanced at the woman and saw her looking at him, her beautiful exotic face composed. As if she didn't remember the one night they'd spent together. How completely she'd surrendered; how perfectly they'd fit.

And how easily she'd betrayed him the next day.

Silhouette

INTIMATE MOMENTS™

presents a riveting new continuity series:

FIRSTBORN SONS

Bound by the legacy of their fathers, these Firstborn Sons are about to discover the stuff true heroes— and true love—are made of!

The adventure continues in November 2001 with:

BORN IN SECRET by Kylie Brant

When Walker James was assigned to infiltrate a terrorist compound and discover the location of a deadly virus, the suave international spy was less than thrilled to be teamed up with Jasmine LeBarr. He'd tangled with the clever secret agent once before, and her covert maneuvers had done a hatchet job on his macho pride. Come hell or high water, he was not about to cave in to their sizzling desire ever again! Or so he thought....

July: **BORN A HERO**
by **Paula Detmer Riggs** (IM #1088)
August: **BORN OF PASSION**
by **Carla Cassidy** (IM #1094)
September: **BORN TO PROTECT**
by **Virginia Kantra** (IM #1100)
October: **BORN BRAVE**
by **Ruth Wind** (IM #1106)
November: **BORN IN SECRET**
by **Kylie Brant** (IM #1112)
December: **BORN ROYAL**
by **Alexandra Sellers**
(IM #1118)

*Available only from
Silhouette Intimate Moments
at your favorite retail outlet.*

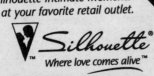

Silhouette®
Where love comes alive™

Visit Silhouette at www.eHarlequin.com

SIMFIRST5

If you enjoyed what you just read,
then we've got an offer you can't resist!

Take 2 bestselling love stories FREE!

Plus get a FREE surprise gift!

Clip this page and mail it to Silhouette Reader Service™

IN U.S.A.
3010 Walden Ave.
P.O. Box 1867
Buffalo, N.Y. 14240-1867

IN CANADA
P.O. Box 609
Fort Erie, Ontario
L2A 5X3

YES! Please send me 2 free Silhouette Intimate Moments® novels and my free surprise gift. After receiving them, if I don't wish to receive anymore, I can return the shipping statement marked cancel. If I don't cancel, I will receive 6 brand-new novels every month, before they're available in stores! In the U.S.A., bill me at the bargain price of $3.80 plus 25¢ shipping and handling per book and applicable sales tax, if any*. In Canada, bill me at the bargain price of $4.21 plus 25¢ shipping and handling per book and applicable taxes**. That's the complete price and a savings of at least 10% off the cover prices—what a great deal! I understand that accepting the 2 free books and gift places me under no obligation ever to buy any books. I can always return a shipment and cancel at any time. Even if I never buy another book from Silhouette, the 2 free books and gift are mine to keep forever.

245 SEN DFNU
345 SEN DFNV

Name	(PLEASE PRINT)	
Address	Apt.#	
City	State/Prov.	Zip/Postal Code

* Terms and prices subject to change without notice. Sales tax applicable in N.Y.
** Canadian residents will be charged applicable provincial taxes and GST.
All orders subject to approval. Offer limited to one per household and not valid to current Silhouette Intimate Moments® subscribers.
® are registered trademarks of Harlequin Enterprises Limited.

INMOM01   ©1998 Harlequin Enterprises Limited

Revitalize!

With help from
Silhouette's *New York Times*
bestselling authors
and receive a

FREE

Refresher Kit!

Retail Value of $25.00 U.S.

LUCIA IN LOVE by Heather Graham
and LION ON THE PROWL by Kasey Michaels

LOVE SONG FOR A RAVEN by Elizabeth Lowell
and THE FIVE-MINUTE BRIDE by Leanne Banks

MACKENZIE'S PLEASURE by Linda Howard
and DEFENDING HIS OWN by Beverly Barton

DARING MOVES by Linda Lael Miller
and MARRIAGE ON DEMAND by Susan Mallery

Don't miss out!

*Look for this exciting promotion, on sale in
October 2001 at your favorite retail outlet.
See inside books for details.*

Only from

Where love comes alive™

Visit Silhouette at www.eHarlequin.com   PSNCP-POPR

CALL THE ONES YOU LOVE OVER THE HOLIDAYS!

Save $25 off future book purchases when you buy any four Harlequin® or Silhouette® books in October, November and December 2001,

PLUS

receive a phone card good for 15 minutes of long-distance calls to anyone you want in North America!

WHAT AN INCREDIBLE DEAL!

Just fill out this form and attach 4 proofs of purchase (cash register receipts) from October, November and December 2001 books, and Harlequin Books will send you a coupon booklet worth a total savings of $25 off future purchases of Harlequin® and Silhouette® books, AND a 15-minute phone card to call the ones you love, anywhere in North America.

Please send this form, along with your cash register receipts as proofs of purchase, to:
In the USA: Harlequin Books, P.O. Box 9057, Buffalo, NY 14269-9057
In Canada: Harlequin Books, P.O. Box 622, Fort Erie, Ontario L2A 5X3
Cash register receipts must be dated no later than December 31, 2001.
Limit of 1 coupon booklet and phone card per household.
Please allow 4-6 weeks for delivery.

I accept your offer! Please send me my coupon booklet and a 15-minute phone card:

Name: _____

Address: _____ City: _____

State/Prov.: _____ Zip/Postal Code: _____

Account Number (if available): _____

---

097 KJB DAGL
PHQ4012

COMING NEXT MONTH

SIMCNM1001